THE MAGICIAN

THE SPINSTER TAKES A GROOM

KATHLEEN LAWLESS

Cover design by Sweet'n'Spicy Designs.

ISBN ebook: 978-1-989873-66-3

ISBN print: 978-1-989873-67-0

Praise for Kathleen Lawless

ANORA'S PRIDE: "Four stars!"
~ *Heartland Critiques*

"*CALLIE'S HONOR* is a great western romance."
~ *S. Wurman, Night Owl Reviews (4.5 Stars)*

CALLIE'S HONOR: "Chemistry...steadily simmers until it finally boils over. If you have not been introduced to the works of Kathleen Lawless, this is an excellent place to start... You will not regret it."
~ *C. Bell, Long and Short Romance Reviews (4 Books)*

MADDY'S FUGITIVE "has it all—romance, action, mystery, and solid characters and plot. Tension between Jud and Maddy as well as the mystery surrounding Jud's innocence grabbed my attention and held on tight."
~ *Jen, Romancing the Book (4 Roses)*

"I liked it way too much. Lol!"
~ *Dee, Shameless Romance Reviews (4 Stars)*

MADDY'S FUGITIVE "was a fun, passionate, engaging whodunit with a strong, stubborn heroine. I was quickly drawn in ... an interesting, worthwhile story."
~ *Josie, Night Owl Reviews (4.5 Stars)*

"A fast-paced book that hooks the reader from the very first page."
~ *Anne Black, RT (4 Stars)*

CALLIE'S HONOR: "This heart-warming Western adventure demonstrates convincingly that love is always a risk worth taking."
~ *Romantic Times (3 Stars)*

"Do not miss ... Lawless weaves romance, intrigue, and excitement into an impressive tapestry."
~ *Romance Reviews Today*

"*CALLIE'S HONOR* reminded me of the down-to-earth heroines [of] Pamela Morsi ... Set in Oregon in the mid 1800s ... a heroine ... trying to keep her ranch together and the drifter who has his own agenda."
~ *Cathie Linz, Romantic Times*

Sign up for Kathleen's VIP Reader Newsletter to be updated on new releases or when her books go on a special fan pricing for her readers. http://eepurl.com/bVosbI

Dedication

Dedicated to my own real life hero, Steel
Who affectionately calls me his 'handful'.

PROLOGUE

Ten years earlier...

Chandra snuggled closer to Afi, her grandfather, on the stiff seat of the train, as he sat reading his paper. Her three sisters sat across from them, making mean faces at her when he wasn't looking. They were just jealous because she was Afi's favorite.

She moved closer and put her small hand on his knee. Without looking away from his paper, he patted it with a large white hand, speckled with dark spots.

The girls said they'd been to Silver Springs Junction five years ago, and made fun of her because she didn't remember. Who remembered anything from when they were three?

She blocked out their chatter about what the new town might be like, and if there'd be other kids there. She was glad Miss Lester, their governess, was going with them. Not only did Miss Lester make lessons fun, she was good at making up stories and acting out the parts, something

Chandra tried to copy. Her sisters laughed at her efforts, but Miss Lester said she had a gift for pretending.

Chandra sighed. If she could pretend to be anyone else, she'd be a little girl with a mom and dad like other children.

CHAPTER 1

Every direction Chandra looked on High Street, the Silver Springs Junction Festival was a smashing success. Which was good news and bad. Good news in that Afi would be in a grand mood and likely to agree to whatever she asked. Bad news in that it meant new settlers would soon be pouring into the town. Settlers sure to include a wave of eligible bachelors eager to align themselves with the granddaughters of the town's wealthy founder.

She'd been horrified when her sister, Selene, relayed a conversation she'd overheard between Afi and his friend, Bolton. Going by what Selene had heard, Bolton was here to help lure prospective grooms to settle in Silver Springs Junction. Outcome; marriage for his granddaughters.

Afi, a nickname the girls adopted for their grandfather after seeing it in a story about Vikings, could be every bit as determined and ruthless as history credited the actual Vikings. If he was determined to marry off her and her sisters, nothing would deter him from that goal.

Chandra shuddered at the thought of married life. Not that she knew much about the holy wedded state other than what she'd been exposed to in her early years. It hadn't mattered whereabouts in the country they traveled. Women were little more than chattel. Doing whatever their husbands dictated. Unpaid cooks, washerwomen, and brood mares, with no lives of their own.

Miss Lester had agreed with her, and right then and there Chandra had set her sights on a different course, the ways and means she was still working out. The solution could be right in front of her, in the form of the handsome young magician, wowing the crowd with his sleight of hand moves and bewitching stunts on stage. She just needed to sell him on her scheme.

The performance ended, and the magician disappeared in a poof of smoke. As the spectators exited out front, Chandra ducked through the back. A short distance behind the performance tent a colorful caravan, belonging to the father and son magic team, was parked. TJ (she'd heard his father call him that and wondered what the initials stood for) sat on the caravan's back steps, his jacket unbuttoned and his tie on the ground next to him. He was drinking straight from a whisky bottle without the nicety of a glass. What a difference from Afi, who maintained whisky tasted much better when served in the proper glassware.

She leaned against the scratchy bark of a nearby pine tree and waited for TJ to notice her among the shadows. It didn't take long. He took another pull on the bottle before he pushed himself to his feet and strode purposefully toward her.

"Show's over," he said curtly.

"So I'm aware."

He struck a match, which flared briefly, illuminating her features and his before it sputtered and went out. His eyes were dark like coal. His cheekbones pronounced, his jaw square. A lock of dark hair, which he constantly pushed aside during his performance, fell across his forehead.

His eyes narrowed. "I've seen you around before."

"I didn't think you'd noticed."

He took another sip from the bottle then, as if remembering his manners, offered it her way. She shook her head.

His mouth twisted cynically. "Isn't it past the princess's bedtime?"

She stiffened. "Don't call me Princess."

"At least I didn't take you for *one of those* females."

"*Those* females?"

"I see them in every town. Usually married. Which doesn't stop them from making a play for me or my Da, depending on their tastes."

Did he mean what she thought he meant? If so, her education of the world was sorely lacking. Something she'd need to set about changing. "How do you know I'm not?"

"Didn't take long to hear all about the town's founding family. A wealthy patron and his four granddaughters."

"What else did you hear?"

"Nothing."

"That's interesting." She tossed her head. "Because I heard you and your father arguing the other evening."

His scowl deepened. "What's it to you?"

"Maybe nothing. Maybe—" She changed the subject abruptly. "How long have you been performing magic tricks?"

He gave a scoffing laugh. "Since I could walk."

"And you're tired of the life." Which had been the crux of the raised voices between TJ and his father. That he didn't want to follow in the old man's footsteps.

His look darkened. She could almost feel his distrust. It rose off of him in waves. "This life is all the old man knows.

But he's too stubborn and proud to admit when it's time to quit."

And TJ wanted something different. Chandra understood. She loved her grandfather and her sisters but none of them had the slightest idea what she was about. Sometimes she wondered if she'd been born into the wrong family. Maia content to run the hotel, Selene obsessed with the gaming hall, and Minerva immersed in her art.

If she had to choose, she'd say she was the most like Minerva. Her sister pined to run away to Paris and study art, but would never make such a move without Afi's blessing. Which she'd never get. Not so long as Afi believed the girls' places were here, bewitching some poor bloke into marriage. Which is why Chandra decided to take control of her own destiny.

"Like I said before, what's it to you if you heard the old man and I arguing? Even wealthy families have their disagreements."

She wouldn't give him the satisfaction of letting him know he was right. Instead, she gave a secret smile before turning on her heel. Her goal, to pique his interest, had been accomplished. "Good evening, TJ. See you tomorrow." She resisted the urge to peek over her shoulder, to see if he was standing there with his mouth hanging open. She hoped he was.

Halfway up the street to the hotel, she ran into Maia and Minerva.

"There you are!" said Maia in her exasperated, big-sister bossy tone. "We were getting ready to send out a search party."

Chandra prayed she was joking. "Just enjoying the energy and success of the festival. Afi must be over the moon."

"He'd be more than over the moon if he had us all safely married off," Maia said. "He worries about us."

She refrained from commenting that Maia worried enough for the entire family. Instead, she linked an arm with each of her sisters before they continued up High Street to where the hotel stood sentry, as if watching over the town and its focal point, the train station.

"How come no one worries about Selene?" she asked. Their absent sister spent her evenings at the newly opened gaming hall across the street from the hotel and no one said a thing.

"Why do you think Afi summoned Beckett here to help her get the hall up and running?" Maia said.

"To keep an eye on Selene?"

"More like make sure she doesn't stumble and fall."

A fact Selene made no secret of royally resenting. Whether she admitted it or not, Selene had been in over her head before the arrival of Afi's friend, Beckett. And even though Selene started out resenting him, the pair had forged some sort of truce. The newly-opened gaming hall was a huge success, one more attraction to lure newcomers into the area. To help fulfill Afi's dream to make Silver Springs Junction the most popular destination in the West.

"Only two more days of the festival," Maia said. "I wouldn't say as much to Afi, but I'm looking forward to things settling down more toward normal."

"I thought you enjoyed the hotel being so busy," Chandra said.

"We're almost too busy," Maia said. "The staff has been run ragged with all the guest requests. We'll all need a few days to recover after the bulk of them leave."

"Including Callan?" Chandra teased, pleased to see a faint pink tinge stain Maia's cheeks.

"The man is insufferable," Maia huffed.

"Much like a certain someone in his employ," Minerva muttered.

"Who's that?" Chandra asked.

Before Minerva could answer, the front doors of the gaming hall burst open. Even though it was dark, enough light spilled from the open doorway for Chandra to make out the shock of white hair belonging to their grandfather. He turned to help his companion, a smartly-dressed older woman, down the steps. On the heels of the first couple were Afi's friend Bolton, a former bounty hunter, and his wife, Lila.

The girls paused, waiting for the others to reach them.

"Trying your luck, were you?" Chandra asked.

Adria, the town's resident widow and busy body, patted Afi's arm. "Your grandfather has been most patient, teaching me some of his best poker moves."

"Adria is a natural," Afi said.

"I've enjoyed learning the game as well," Lila said. "You never know when I might be able to use that information in a book."

"You should talk to Callan while he's here," Afi said. "The man is involved in different aspects of publishing. He might have some useful contacts."

"Speaking of contacts," Lila said. "Does anyone know the origin of the symbols I've seen carved on several of the trees down near the station?"

"Carvings on trees?" Afi's brow wrinkled. "Are you sure you're not letting your writer's imagination get the best of you?"

Lila turned to her husband. "You've seen them."

"I have," Bolton said. But he didn't expand on his answer, and the conversation shifted as their group reached the hotel and Afi invited his guests to join him for a cognac. Chandra and her sisters declined and said their goodnights.

Before they left, Maia singled out Bolton. "I'm counting on you to make sure Afi stops at one."

Afi sputtered and Bolton laughed. Chandra sent Afi a sympathetic look. At least when Maia was acting mother hen to someone else, it took the heat off her.

Chandra and Maia left Minerva at the doorway to the room she shared with Selene and carried on down the hallway to their room.

"Maia," Chandra said, trying to keep her voice studiedly casual. "Afi has holdings in town other than the hotel and the emporium, right?"

"Why do you ask?"

"I was thinking about that warehouse that's near the station. The one by the river that's not being used."

"You know Afi. Always planning for the future. He sees Silver Springs Junction as a major port in the transport of goods from train to river. Ahead of his time as usual."

"That's what I thought." Chandra washed her face and changed into her nightdress. She was already under the covers by the time Maia climbed into her own bed and extinguished the gas lamp on the stand between them. Through the open window the faint sounds of music drifted up the hill from the festival. One thing was for sure. The town wouldn't be the same once the festival performers packed up and left. Since Afi had great vision for the future, she hoped he saw the merit in her proposal.

CHAPTER 2

Try as he might, TJ couldn't rid himself of the memory of the way the young woman smirked at him before she left. He'd seen her with her sisters during the festival's early days, but lately she'd come alone to watch the show, a serious look on her face. He imagined her giving her sisters the slip, and wondered how that went over. Or had she spent her entire life doing whatever she wanted, indulged and pampered? Seemed more likely.

He stared to where the hotel looked down on the town. Right now, it was a black shadow against even blacker mountains, but in daylight it glowed with a life of its own. Cut granite blocks formed the exterior walls while sunlight glinted off the mullioned, over-height windows. Not exactly the type of place he or Pa were ever likely to frequent.

He laid away the half-empty bottle before he was tempted to finish it. After one last look toward the mountains, he climbed the few narrow steps to the caravan that had been his home as long as he could remember. Of course, no place had felt like home after Ma ran off. He'd been young; his last memory the three of them on stage.

How radiant and beautiful she was, all eyes upon her. Him and pa had adored her.

Which made her leaving such a shock. One day she was simply gone. He never saw pa smile again, and neither of them ever mentioned her name. By the time he hit his teens, he was already tired of their life. As they chased their tails from one side of the country to the other, he could almost understand why his ma took off. Understand maybe. Forgive? Never.

Which didn't stop him from looking for a way out. That girl had been right. Not only was he tired of the nomadic lifestyle, he was worried about the toll it was taking on Pa. The old man was plumb tired and worn out. He might kick and scream if TJ ever declared they were staying put, but likely wouldn't fight for long. TJ suspected he might even be relieved.

Trouble was, what would they do? Neither of them would be happy on a little spread of land where they could park the caravan for the last time and pasture the horses. Already, he was dreading the festival's end. The packing up. The aimless journey down whatever road ran close to the rail line. Eventually they'd reach a new town, a new place to set up their act.

Inside the caravan, Pa was snoring loud enough to shake the roof off the ancient conveyance. TJ grabbed his bedroll and headed for the hammock he'd strung between two trees back of the caravan. As a precaution, he picked up his rifle. One never knew out here.

THAT GIRL WAS BACK. Not that he'd been watching for her. He'd been in the middle of his act when he suddenly felt her gaze. He looked over and sure enough— Okay, if truth be told, he *had* been wondering when he'd see her again.

As daylight helped illuminate the tent's interior, he reassessed his earlier opinion. She was no girl, rather every inch a woman. Laughing dark eyes that had likely never known struggles or disappointments met his. An obviously expensive green gown made the most of her feminine attributes without revealing more than was seemly. Beneath a jaunty hat, her dark hair was piled atop her head in a fetching way that revealed the long, slender column of her neck and throat, while full red lips begged for a man's kiss. He wondered if she'd ever been kissed. Tempting to find out.

As the act drew to a close, he bowed amidst a polite spatter of applause and hopped down off the front of the stage. He strode through the dispersing crowd as if they weren't even there, eyes for her alone.

He reached her side, his gaze raking her form from toe to head and back again before finally settling on her face. Her skin had the consistency of newly separated cream. Her lashes were thick and dark and fringed her eyes. This close, he saw their whisky depths were shot with threads of gold.

Rather than appearing intimidated by his bold scrutiny, she countered the move, a faint smile playing with those luscious lips, as if she approved of what she saw. With a start, he realized they were the only two left inside the tent. His heart skipped. He could always tell when a woman wanted something, and this one was no different. Disappointment rippled through him. He'd wanted her to be different.

She inclined her head toward the tent's entrance. "Take a walk?"

"Where to?" The caravan perhaps?

"Down near the station. There's something I want to show you."

Broad daylight. People milling about. Perhaps he'd misjudged her after all.

"Not until you tell me your name."

"It's Chandra Crawford. And you're TJ. Which stands for...?"

"Not even my close friends know that." Who was he kidding? He had no close friends. Moving around since the day he'd been born wasn't conducive to fostering friendships, let alone anything more. He'd had his share of women over the years, faceless, nameless bodies who came to him in the dark and left before daylight. All of which was fine by him.

"Well, TJ. Thank you for indulging me," she said as they filtered through the festival goers crowding the streets. He bit back a laugh. It was obvious she was accustomed to being indulged.

"Did I have a choice?"

She cocked him a look. "One always has a choice."

"Let's just say you piqued my interest. Women rarely choose to be seen with me in broad daylight."

She laughed. "Obviously you're consorting with the wrong kinds of women."

Women from his own league. A league which did not include a lady like Chandra.

"What do you do besides observe magic shows and eavesdrop on family disputes?"

"I think I'll save that for a bit. First, let's see how you react to what I plan to show you."

As they walked together down High Street, he was surprised at the lack of attention they drew. He'd been expecting people to stare and point, wondering what a man like him was doing with a woman like her. But they could have been any two festival goers.

At the end of High Street, they crossed the bridge to the train station with its zig-zag of track. Rail lines merging from Northern, mid, and Southern states all met in one messy-looking snarl. Scattered out of sight through the scrubby woods on both sides of the riverbank, hidden camps were populated by men who rode the rails in search of a better life. If one even existed.

Beyond the station, just past the bridge, sat a lonely-looking structure. Relatively new, no sign identified the building or its purpose. His eyes widened as Chandra pulled a large iron key from her reticule and approached the double front door.

"What is this place?" No hinges squeaked as she pushed open one of the doors and he moved to help before following her in. Streaks of sunlight filtered through the open doorway, illuminating the way their feet stirred dust motes on the wooden plant floor.

"*This* is what I wanted to show you."

"I don't understand."

"My grandfather built this to be a warehouse. It's been sitting empty ever since." Arms out, she spun in a circle. "Don't you think it would make a simply amazing theater?"

As he took in their surroundings, a sudden image beamed into his brain. He envisioned a large center stage, tables and chairs on all sides. Strategically placed steps led from the main floor to a raised level, elevated viewing for patrons near the back.

"Is that what your grandfather intends to do with it?"

She gave him a cocky smile. "It will be once I get done with him. With your help, of course."

"My help? I—"

"You said yourself you've been in show business all your life. I need someone with your experience to convince him it's a viable idea."

TJ's image dissipated as clearly as a soap bubble bursting. "You have the wrong man."

"I think not." She sashayed up to him. "Not only are you bright and energetic, you understand the business. And you're spoiling for a change."

How did she know that? "What's your role in all this?"

"A means to what *I* want. A career on the stage. One which eventually takes me away from here. To New York City."

She was serious!

He blew out a breath. He'd heard the rich were different. This spoiled rich girl had no idea what she was up against. No idea what the life she thought she wanted entailed.

Ironic, the way humans always seem to hanker after whatever they don't have. Chandra had the financial security and stable life that had been forever out of his reach. Something she was ready to turn her back on for the supposed glamor of a career on stage. If she only knew! Still, it wasn't up to him to educate her. She'd figure it out eventually. In the meantime, he and pa could put down roots.

He could see it already. Instead of spending grueling hours performing, Pa could take a break and teach a few tricks to any folks willing to put down hard-earned cash for the privilege. TJ could manage the theater, book the acts. Make a name for himself.

His cynical side reminded him that when things sound too good to be true, they usually are.

He eyed Chandra. Was she playing with him? Baiting him with something he wanted, only to change her mind and lose interest at the last minute when something newer and shinier came along?

"What you're talking about doesn't happen overnight. Do you have any idea how much work is involved?"

Chandra managed to look insulted and disappointed at the same time. "I watched my sister turn a chunk of raw land into the fanciest, most elegant gaming hall in the West. I expect this'll be a lot less work."

"What guarantee do I have that you won't lose interest partway through?"

Her eyes narrowed. "Is that what you base your decision-making on? Guarantees? I gave you credit for more spunk than that."

Her words took him aback. She sounded like she believed in him. "You seem pretty convinced your grandfather will go along with the idea."

She gave her head a toss the same way he'd seen a spirited filly do. Maybe there was more to this cossetted rich girl than met the eye. "You just leave Afi to me. He's never said 'no' to me yet. And I know exactly how to sell him on the idea."

Reluctantly, he heard himself agree to give her his answer by the time the festival ended.

CHAPTER 3

Chandra's impatience flared along with the ostentatious display of fireworks lighting up the sky. Still no word from TJ. Was he afraid to face her? She paced back and forth between the tent and the caravan, but neither TJ nor his father appeared. Afi's scheme to wind up the week-long festival with a stunning display of fireworks had been sheer genius. Her grandfather never did anything by half measures, but had his own personal crew to set off the display. Like the festival itself, the fireworks show had been nothing but spectacular.

Now the fireworks and the festival were over. Except for Afi's Festival's End party, where she was expected to make an appearance. Right now, the last thing she wanted to do was spark Afi's displeasure. After a final look around, as if half-expecting TJ to pop out from behind a tree, she headed back. Her feet dragged as she followed the straggly parade of people trudging along the darkened street, her eyes scanning the crowd for a glimpse of TJ.

Eventually she reached the hotel, where the men in attendance outnumbered women in a high ratio. How many of the newcomers were potential suitors for her and her sisters? Those new in town stuck out from the town's early settlers and the festival performers, who mostly mingled among themselves. Everywhere she looked, guests were gazing around the hotel's grand lobby with awe, taking in the soaring ceilings, marble columns, fancy windows and grand central staircase.

She'd never been much of one for parties. Drifting through the lobby, trying not to make eye contact with anyone, she imagined herself in character from one of the books of stage plays she had managed to get her hands on. A grieving widow. Across the room she spotted TJ's father near the piano, performing card tricks for the guests gathered around to watch. But no sign of TJ.

She was on her way to inquire as to his son's whereabouts when Maia caught sight of her and bustled over. Chandra sighed. So much for imaging herself as someone else. Time to put on her party face. And forget about TJ.

"Trust you to miss all the excitement," Maia said.

"It looks exciting enough to me," Chandra said in a sarcastic Southern drawl, that of a different character she'd been practicing.

Maia didn't seem to notice. "If you weren't so self-centered, you'd know what's been going on right under your nose. The Mathers kidnapped Beckett and tried to burn him alive in an old shack."

Chandra did a double-take. Had Maia been nipping into Afi's special stash of whisky? "Are you serious? The preacher?"

"Turns out he wasn't a preacher, but a man with a vendetta against Beckett and Afi. All of us, really. Who knows what might have happened if they'd run into you out there on your own."

Could the Mathers have seen her with TJ? Grabbed him up as a way to further their vendetta?

She gave her head a faint shake. No good would come from letting her imagination take hold. TJ was likely holed up somewhere with a bottle of whisky for company. After all, they hadn't set a firm day and time for his answer.

"Anyway, the pair showed up here dressed in clown costumes and Mathers pulled out a rifle. Thank goodness Beckett managed to disarm him—"

"I thought Beckett was being burned alive?" This story was getting crazier by the second.

"Oh, he escaped," Maia said breezily. "And came back to warn us all."

"Thank goodness for that." Chandra glanced around for one of her other sisters for support. Maia's convoluted story was hard to believe, especially given the way the party continued on around them. Luckily, Minerva must have seen her plea for help and joined them.

"Thank goodness you're all right! The Mathers have been on a rampage against our whole family and we were concerned you might have fallen into harm's way."

So Maia's story wasn't total fabrication. "Where are the culprits now?"

"Oh, Bolton had the sheriff on side. He's carted them off."

"Thank goodness for Bolton," Chandra said, still with a twinge of sarcasm. Her sisters were prone to exaggeration and she'd bet this was one of those times.

"Oh, there's Selene, now," Minerva said. "She was relieved to learn Beckett didn't run off the way it appeared."

"Beckett and Selene?" The pair didn't even like each other. Had she fallen down a rabbit hole like poor hapless Alice, into a world where things no longer made sense? She gave her head another shake in an effort to clear it. "I'd best go mingle before everyone leaves."

It must be later than she thought, for as she'd been talking to the girls the crowd started to thin. Afi was nowhere to be seen. Not that this was the right moment to approach him with her idea, anyway. Especially given the recent drama. She sighed. Suddenly she felt like a stranger in her own home. Behind her, Maia was telling the staff to leave the cleanup until the morning. Which was very un-Maia-like.

Selene hadn't moved. Chandra turned and followed her gaze to the closed door of Afi's study. Peculiar! This entire evening had a surreal air, like that of a dream. Abruptly the study door opened and Beckett appeared. He swooped past her to Selene and swept her up in his arms, his grin a mile wide. Hardly the behavior of someone who'd been kidnapped and nearly killed, then rallied to apprehend the villains. The whole preposterous story sounded like something from a bad dime novel.

"It took some doing," Beckett said to Selene. "But Crawford finally gave me his blessing."

"Wonderful!" To Chandra's amazement, Selene pressed her lips to his in full view of everyone before she turned to face her sisters. "How do you three feel about being bridesmaids at my wedding?"

"As if you'd have anyone else," Maia said with a sniff. "Which of us will be your maid of honor?"

"All of you," Selene said, laughing happily as Beckett linked his fingers through hers and tugged her toward the balcony.

Chandra blinked. No one else was showing the slightest surprise at this latest turn of events.

"When did all this come about?"

Maia arched a brow. "Asks the girl who's been in her own little world since the festival started."

"I've been here along," she retorted, aware it was only half true. She'd been consumed by plans for her future. The first step of which was to secure the cooperation of TJ. Where was the blasted man?

~

TJ DISMANTLED the timeworn canvas tent and folded it carefully, as he had done countless times over the years. His father watched with a critical eye. In past years Pa would have been here alongside him, doing his share, but in the last year or so he'd been content to settle onto a nearby stump or chunk of firewood and issue orders. Orders TJ ignored. He'd done this so often he could do it in his sleep.

"Smooth the corner, boy. It has to fit in that special cubby behind the wheel."

Where it always went. As he worked, TJ kept one eye out for Chandra. He had little doubt she'd hunt him down and demand an answer to her proposition. Had probably expected it last evening and was steamed when she couldn't find him.

He'd tossed and turned all night, changing his mind from one minute to the next. It would be good for Pa to slow down, to stay put for a change. Not so good for him to be handcuffed to Chandra, subject to her every whim. Nothing to stop her from changing her mind before the theater was finished. Or use him to get the theater ready, then decide she no longer needed him involved.

He'd been raised to distrust women. And learned early on that life held no guarantees. Was that same distrust blinding him to a golden opportunity right under his nose?

He didn't much believe in prayer, but if he did, this could well be the answer to his.

As if he'd conjured her in his thoughts, he turned to see Chandra talking to his old man. He hurried to join them before she could speak out of turn.

"I was just congratulating your father for his part in entertaining my grandfather's guests last night at the after party." Her cool look matched her cool tone. "It's a shame you weren't there to see him. He was in his element."

So, she was bugged by his disappearing act after the festival. He'd been down at the hobo camp, checking on some of the men he knew from way back, confident she'd never look for him there. Meanwhile her words had turned his pa's stubbly, unshaven cheeks pink. Couldn't he see Chandra was just buttering him up?

She directed her attention to TJ. "My grandfather would like to thank you personally for your contribution to the festival. Would you be able to meet with us at the hotel this afternoon?"

"Of course he would." Pa spoke before he could answer for himself. "It would be an honor." He nodded approvingly in TJ's direction. "Isn't that right, boy?"

He cringed. Pa had been calling him 'boy' since his first time on stage. And even though he'd hit manhood years ago, the habit persisted. He ran his gaze over Chandra, in yet another expensive frock, her hair tucked up beneath an elaborate and fashionable matching hat. The thought of the two of them in some sort of partnership was laughable. And yet— Maybe it was time she learned about hard work and the ways of the world. How life was for those less fortunate.

He gave a curt nod. "I'll be there." Then he turned back to what he'd been doing.

As CHANDRA HAD ANTICIPATED, Afi was in a tremendously jolly mood following the festival's success. Alone with him in his study, she listened patiently as he expounded on his plans for the following year.

"Your sister is pestering me to invite a group of artists to attend next year. I suppose it wouldn't hurt to humor her."

Good. He was in a mood to humor.

"I had a similar thought," she said with studied casualness.

Afi frowned. "Don't tell me you have a yen to run off and study art with Minerva?"

"Hardly," Chandra said. "But I've been so impressed seeing what Selene accomplished with the emporium, I happened upon an idea for my own special project. One that will also ignite interest in the town."

"You might as well spill it," Afi said amicably. "I can see I'll get no peace until I've at least heard you out."

"Yes, well you know how Selene and Beckett worked past their differences for the good of the gaming hall?"

"You've not developed a sudden interest in games of chance, have you?"

"You could say that. But not in the way you're thinking."

TJ MADE a point of not craning his neck to stare up at the impressive sweep of soaring ceilings in the hotel lobby. He shoved his hands in his pockets and pretended he was used to things like grand pianos, glittering gaslight sconces, and rugs underfoot that felt softer than his sleeping pallet. Well-to-do guests brushed past him as if he didn't exist. Further proof that he'd never fit in, not even in his best jacket and hat.

Chandra had left him to cool his heels while she spoke to her grandfather first. 'Smooth the way' was how she'd put it. She'd indicated the settee against the far wall, but he'd chosen to remain on his feet, moving about as if he did it every day and had every right to be here.

His head jerked and his shoulders tensed at the sound of a nearby door opening. He turned as Chandra crossed the lobby to his side. He should have met her halfway but his feet felt rooted to the fancy carpet.

Smiling, she took his hand. "Our turn."

How did she do that? Talk about them together. As if this whole crazy idea of hers was a done-deal. Suddenly, he realized he wanted it. This chance to change the trajectory of his life.

He pulled on his devil-may-care face that had seen him through many a challenging situation. "Shouldn't I go in alone?"

"That's not a good idea. Since I plan to be closely involved, it's important Afi understand that from the start." Which made sense. Sort of. Or did it?

His eyes narrowed. What was she up to? Her own eyes were focused near her feet, avoiding his gaze. He pulled up short, tugging on her arm. "What's going on? What aren't you telling me?"

"N—nothing. Come on. We don't want to keep Afi waiting."

He'd seen Crawford around the festival over the past week, but only from a distance. Up close, despite his white hair and advanced years, the man exuded a presence. As if he knew things other folks didn't. Perhaps that was his secret to success.

"Afi. This is TJ, the young man I was telling you about." After presenting him as if to royalty, she moved around the massive mahogany desk to stand to one side behind her grandfather, hands clasped behind her back. Was their side of the desk for family, his for visitors?

Crawford rose and reached across his desk to shake TJ's hand. His grip was firm and strong. If TJ hadn't known better, he'd have said he was shaking hands with a much younger man.

"Mr. Crawford," TJ said respectfully. He'd knocked around enough to have picked up some manners from folks more well-schooled than him.

"Call me Crawford like everyone else. What does TJ stand for?"

"A mother's whimsy," he said with a self-deprecating smile as he met Crawford's gaze squarely. If they were going to be business partners, the older man needed to know TJ could hold his own.

"Good answer," Crawford said, plucking at the knees of his trousers as he sat back down. TJ did likewise, mimicking the man's actions. Chandra remained standing.

"Now what's all this I hear about you and my granddaughter?"

His eyes flew to Chandra who sent him an encouraging nod.

"Chandra is a woman with her own ideas, and that's for sure."

Crawford barked out a laugh. "You figured that out pretty quick." He glanced from one to the other. "I have to say, this came on so sudden I had my doubts. But Chandra has convinced me it's not an impulsive move on the part of either of you."

TJ fell silent for a moment. "No, sir. I wouldn't call it impulsive. I feel it bodes well for both of our futures."

He had a sense of Crawford taking his measure.

"The important thing is, and I know Chandra agrees with me on this," Crawford said, "is that there's no rush."

"I'd hate to see things drag on, but I'm a firm believer it's important to get it right the first time."

"I couldn't agree more," Crawford said. "Setting the tone for your future."

"Exactly."

Crawford waved an expansive hand through the air. "I'd say this calls for a drink. Chandra, fetch the decanter and two glasses if you don't mind."

Chandra plucked the requested items from the sideboard and placed them in front of her grandfather. The old man poured a generous two fingers into each glass and slid one toward him. When he rose to pick it up, Crawford also rose, lifting his glass toward TJ's. "To the future of you two young people."

TJ obligingly clinked his glass against Crawford's, then took a sip. The whisky was smoother and mellower than anything he'd ever tasted, sliding down his throat like a cloud of liquid silk. Eyes wide, he studied the amber liquid in his glass.

"You approve?" Crawford watched him closely. He felt the way he responded would be key.

"Most excellent, sir. Thank you."

Crawford nodded. "I always say you can tell a lot about a man by his taste in whisky." Crawford's brows drew tightly together. His scrutiny left TJ feeling like a bug under a microscope. "Even though it goes against my better judgement, Chandra caught me in a mellow mood. I accept your suit, and congratulate you both on your betrothal. Welcome to the family."

He nearly choked in shock. Behind Crawford, Chandra nodded her head, one finger to her lips in a silent gesture for him to hold his tongue. He pressed his lips together in a tight line. He'd been right not to trust her. What game was she playing? He tossed back the rest of his drink, biding his time.

"Now that that's settled." Crawford eased back into his chair while TJ remained standing, his eyes shooting daggers over the old man's head toward Chandra. "You have my blessing to turn that white elephant of a warehouse into some sort of theater or amusement arcade. I'll have my lawyers draw something up so we all know where we stand."

"Thank you, Afi." Chandra flew to the old man's side and flung her arms around his neck, plastering his cheek with kisses.

Crawford gave a pleased chuckle. "Now both of you, get out of here and let me get some work done."

"Come along, TJ. We have lots of planning to do."

Taking the whisky glass from his hand, Chandra placed it on the table near the door before she pushed him into the lobby and closed the door behind them.

He turned on her. "What the—"

"Not here," she hissed, prodding him across the lobby, outside the front door and across the drive.

"We're not getting married!" He kept his voice deliberately low and forceful.

"No, we're not," Chandra said.

"So do you mind explaining why I was just welcomed into the family?"

She remained silent, her gaze roving across his face.

Eyes narrowed, he crossed his arms, waiting.

She cleared her throat. "I was worried you wouldn't play along if you knew beforehand."

"Dead to rights!"

She blew out a breath. "Afi has this unfortunate bee in his bonnet about seeing my sisters and I settled down into marriage."

"Doesn't sound unreasonable."

"Except I have no intention of every marrying. By pretending to be betrothed, I'll be spared from any of his matching making schemes."

He unfolded his arms. "Say I go along with this charade. What happens next? Sooner or later, someone is going to expect us to tie the knot."

She made a dismissive gesture with her hands. "Afi will be so busy getting the others married off, by the time we tell him we changed our minds it'll be too late. The theater will be going strong, and with any luck, I'll be on a train East. You can act as heartbroken by my leaving as you care to."

"In the meantime, you and I are to act smitten around each other when the family is present?"

She nodded. "And we both get what we want."

He cocked his head appraisingly. "You're accustomed to getting things your way, aren't you?"

Her shrug and half-smile revealed a part dimple. She peeked out at him from beneath half-lowered lashes. "Usually."

"It sounds like you've thought this all through."

"I didn't sleep a wink last night," she said. "I was studying it from all angles. Figuring the best way to break the news to Afi."

TJ took his time with his response. She was looking a little too smug, like it never occurred to her he might balk.

"Tell you what. I'll play along with your little scheme. On one condition."

"Name it."

"You're going to get a little taste of what life is really like. Guaranteed to enhance your acting skills."

"That sounds reasonable. What do I have to do?"

"You're going to cook up a big pot of beans, along with a batch of corn bread."

She laughed. "Oh, I don't cook. But I'm sure Cook at the hotel—"

He interrupted with a head shake. "No cook. Just you. First you figure out what you need and purchase the supplies over at the General Store. Then you commandeer the hotel's kitchen when no one is around to 'help you'."

Her eyes narrowed to slits. She blew out a breath expressing her disapproval of his terms. "What do you expect me to do with this food once it's prepared?"

"You'll find out."

"And if I refuse?"

"Your grandfather learns you're a liar."

CHAPTER 4

Bolton had been dreading this audience with Crawford. His old friend would want to know what progress he had made in finding potential grooms for the girls, and the truth was none. The type of men heading West to seek their fortunes were not the types Crawford wanted to break bread with at family dinners.

He suspected Crawford was secretly hoping Bolton would dredge up a modern-day version of Crawford in his younger years. Closest Bolton had seen around these parts was Callan Douglas. And even though the newspaper mogul and Crawford had conspired together to bring down the mutual nemesis Frankson, neither man trusted the other. Which was smart.

Bolton well recalled what Crawford had been like when they first met. A less-polished version of Douglas. If someone like that were to show up with wooing on his mind, Crawford would likely show them the door post-haste, with a boot print on their backside. Crawford's daughter had obediently married the man Crawford chose. Someone meek and mild that he could mold and manipulate. No way the girls Crawford raised would settle for someone like that.

"Come!" Crawford barked in response to his knock.

"You're looking like the cat that swallowed the canary. And rightly so. The festival was an unprecedented success."

Crawford took off his glasses and polished them with a handkerchief. "That was yesterday. Today, I've just had a most interesting chin-wag with my youngest."

"Chandra." He didn't know her as well as the others, but from the little he'd seen, she was as stubborn and head-strong as Crawford himself.

"Seems she's found herself a suitor," Crawford said.

"That's—good?" He felt like he was walking into a care-fully baited trap.

"Let's just say that for now she'll be busy and out of trou-ble," Crawford said. "In the meantime, I want you to find out everything you can about the man. Name of TJ Dirks. A magician by trade, allegedly. He and his father were here for the festival and now they're fixing to stay."

"A magician?" The poor fellow had better have more than the usual magician's tricks up his sleeve to pass muster with Crawford.

"Not in the least bit suitable, of course. But I know my blood well enough to know that if I balked at the young man's intentions, it would only push her harder into his waiting arms."

"Opportunist?" Bolton guessed.

"At the least. Dig me up some dirt. Something I can use to quietly run him out of town and out of our lives."

"I'll see what I can find out. You must be pleased about Selene."

Crawford flashed a conspiratorial grin. "Played that one well, didn't I?"

"Like a master. I don't know why you've tasked me with parading a selection of suitors before the girls."

"To bring them to their senses," Crawford growled. "They are getting far too comfortable on their own."

"I don't know about comfortable. Maia fusses around this hotel like it's her child, and *you* created that monster. Something must be going on with Chandra to accept the suit of some traveling trickster. As for Minerva, she seems to be in her own little world. Her and her art."

"I plan to shake her out of that," Crawford said. "Like Chandra and the magician fellow, I'm pretending to support their fanciful dreams. Minerva has it in her head to do something at next year's festival. Something she calls a group of 'artists-in-residence'."

"I've heard of that," Bolton said. "It's not a terrible idea."

"Once she sees what a flakey lot artists can be, it should turn her attention to a more stable sort of fellow. Assuming you've unearthed someone suitable by then."

Bolton listened with half an ear. His brain had locked on a single word. Magician. He'd recently remarked to his wife that it seemed the hotel's mystery thief was some sort of magician, the way they got in and out of guests' rooms with no one being the wiser.

Maybe— No. The thefts started months before the festival. Unless this TJ and his father had been camped nearby for some time. Then took advantage of the festival to make their presence seen.

"So, if this magician fellow intends to stick around and woo Chandra, how will he support himself? Or is he looking for a handout?"

"He and Chandra concocted some harebrain scheme. They intend to turn that unused warehouse down by the river into some sort theater or amusement arcade."

Bolton raised a brow. "With your blessing?"

"What could I say? I endorsed Selene's little venture with the gaming hall. I couldn't very well tell Chandra she couldn't take over a building that's standing idle. Not if I plan to have any influence in her future. This way her time is occupied and she's easy to keep an eye on."

"Her magician will likely prove to be a different kettle of fish."

"Agreed." Crawford said.

"Will this father and son magic act be your guests here at the hotel?"

Crawford snorted. "Over my dead body. There's only so far I'm willing to bend."

Privately, Bolton thought the bending had barely started, at least as far as Chandra and her sisters went. But it wasn't his place to say so. "I'll put out some inquiries," he said. "But, be warned. I expect it will take some time to hear anything. If there's anything to hear."

"That's fine," Crawford said. "For now, he can amuse himself dealing with Chandra and her plans for the warehouse."

CHANDRA WAS IN THE LIBRARY, going over the opening act of a play she was trying to write. She sighed and looked up, drumming her fingertips on the table, already wondering if she'd bitten off more than she could chew with TJ. What on earth made her think he'd meekly play along with her charade?

She heard her sisters before she saw them, Maia leading the charge.

"Flo saw her go into the main library. And here she is."

She looked up to see the three of them crowding the doorway.

Maia looked stern. Minerva looked hurt. As for Selene, Chandra had never been able to read Selene accurately, and given she just announced her own betrothal, she might feel Chandra was stealing her thunder.

The three of them advanced as if one person, all speaking at the same time.

"I knew nothing good would come of you—"

"When were you going to—"

"Is it true?"

She stood to meet them on even ground.

"I was planning to tell you at supper when we were all together. Afi has a big mouth."

"Actually, Maia heard it from Lila. Bolton told her," Selene said.

"Word certainly travels fast." Chandra gave a smug half-smile, followed by a shrug. "Surprise!"

Minerva's frown deepened. "Chandra are you quite sure? You can't have known the man but a few hours."

"Have you never heard of love at first sight?" She had her story prepared. "We each felt as if we were hit by a bolt of lightning. When we started to talk it felt like we've known each other forever. Not only that, it turns out we both share the same dream. What is that, if not some sort of divine intervention from our dear, departed mama?"

Maia made a scoffing sound of disbelief. "Someone has been reading those dime novels again. Lasting love doesn't hit you over the head. It grows over time."

"So you won't object when Afi chooses whom you should marry? Someone he feels is a suitable mate, even if you don't fancy the fellow."

"I didn't say that," Maia said. "Look at Selene. She and Beckett couldn't stand the sight of each other to start with."

"I prefer to start my romantic attachment on a different note," Chandra said.

Minerva pulled up a nearby chair. "So, what's he like? This magician of yours?"

Chandra thought quickly. Not the right moment to admit she hadn't a clue. "As you saw from his act, he's very captivating. Not to mention handsome."

"Are you sure he didn't set his sights on you because of who you are? And set out to sweep you off your feet?"

Chandra laughed. "Quite sure. I practically had to chase him down."

Minerva gasped. "Chandra! You didn't throw yourself at him?"

"Never. In fact, we haven't even kissed."

Selene raised a brow. "That's a problem in itself."

Chandra gave her a level look. "How long did you know Beckett before he kissed you?"

Selene blushed. "We weren't even interested in each other. He was very bold."

"Hmmph. Well TJ is a perfect gentleman."

"What does TJ stand for?" Maia asked

Chandra laughed. "Afi asked him that very thing. He said something about a fanciful mother."

"In other words, you don't even know the full name of the man you intend to marry." This from Minerva.

Chandra rose and gathered up her papers. "I know everything I need to know. He's devoted to his father."

"So what's this plan you and he schemed up together?" Selene asked.

She plopped back into her chair, and the others followed

suit. This felt more like the sisterhood she'd grown up with. "You know Afi's warehouse down by the station? Here's what we intend to do." No need for them to know anything about TJ's ridiculous condition. Have her become some sort of scullery maid. Once they were busy converting the warehouse, he'd be too distracted to even remember. She hoped.

CHAPTER 5

Chandra glared over at TJ. "What have you done with Cook and her helper?" She'd been counting on Cook's guidance, if not her actual assistance.

"I made her disappear," TJ said with a smirk.

After escorting her to the mercantile with a shopping list, he'd been waiting in the kitchen when she returned. She slammed down her purchases for which she'd had to use her own money. It would be impossible to explain to Selene, who posted the hotel accounts, why she was buying dried beans, cornmeal, molasses, eggs and butter. She didn't even know why herself. A quick look through one of Cook's massive books of recipes left her no further enlightened as to how one went about turning her purchases into something edible.

He watched her unload her basket and lay the parcels on the table, clearly enjoying this far too much.

"When are you planning to tell me what this is in aid of?"

"All in good time. I took the liberty of stoking the stove so it would be ready."

"How big of you."

"See that black pot hanging near the stove? You need to first fill that with water."

"I knew that." Actually, she had no clue. If TJ hadn't been here, she might have—what? She glared again at TJ. This was all his fault. She lifted the pot off the hook, unprepared when the weight of it sent it crashing to the floor, nearly ripping her shoulder from its socket at the same time. How did Cook manage such a beast?

As she bent to heft it into the sink, she snuck a look his way. Yup. He was enjoying this no end.

She grabbed the handle of the pump and started working it. Which was harder than it looked. When she stopped to peer inside, she was dismayed to see the water barely covered the bottom of the pot. The heat from the stove made the kitchen uncomfortably warm, and she slicked away the perspiration beading on her forehead. Her sore shoulder complained about this new exertion.

"How full does the pot need to be?"

"Don't you know?"

Grrrr.....

Of course she didn't.

"Half should do."

After what felt like forever, she deemed the pot to be half full and tried to lift it out of the sink, conscious of TJ watching her struggles. She gritted her teeth. No way was she about to break down and ask for his help. Finally, she had it situated.

"Don't forget a pinch of salt before you put the lid on," TJ said casually.

A pinch. Exactly how much was a pinch?

She'd die before she asked.

Salt added, lid in place, she stood back and dusted off

her hands, feeling inordinately pleased by her accomplishments. She didn't dare tell TJ she had no clue what to do next.

"Now you wait for it to boil before you add in the beans."

That made sense. They'd been rock hard when the shop keeper weighed and wrapped them.

"Can you guess what's next?"

"Tea time?" she said hopefully.

TJ laughed uproariously.

Chandra didn't think it was funny at all. An afternoon cup of tea always gave her a lift.

"The oven should be hot enough that you can mix up and bake the cornbread."

If the oven got any hotter, she was going to melt. She cast a baleful look his way. How could he appear so cool and composed?

"I suggest you start by creaming the butter."

Creaming the butter. What did that even mean?

"In a bowl. With the wooden spoon," TJ added helpfully.

Which turned out to be far more difficult than it sounded. She was happy to set the wooden spoon down as the water started boiling. She reached for the lid.

"Wait!" TJ's sharp retort, made her pull back and turn his way. "You can't touch it with your bare hands."

"Oh."

"See that hook on the wall next to the pots?"

She'd always wondered what it was for. Apparently, it was used for lifting hot pot lids. She wielded it like a weapon, her movements clumsy as the lid clattered to the stove. A whoosh of steam hit her full in the face.

"Careful!" TJ pulled her back a step. "Let the steam dissipate."

She turned to him and stamped her foot. "Are you

happy? Point proven? I'm useless at domestic chores. A menace in the kitchen to myself and anyone who happens to be in the way."

He crossed his arms over his chest. "I never took you for a quitter."

Her eyes narrowed. Chandra Crawford was nobody's quitter! And TJ Dirks was not being let off the hook that easily. He was her fake fiancé! Being offered a life-changing opportunity, thanks to her. Something she planned to remind him of at every turn. Once whatever he'd hoped to prove with this kitchen nonsense was behind her.

CHANDRA WAS STUBBORN, a trait TJ had counted on. He had no intention of starting a venture with someone who quit at the first sign of strife, or ran home to have grandpa fix whatever was too difficult for her to deal with. He quite enjoyed seeing this side of her, flushed, mussed, and completely out of her element.

Under his tutelage, with the addition of copious scoops of molasses, the beans were close to edible. The cornbread was nothing to write home about, but it would fill an empty belly. Chandra had only burned herself once pulling the hot pans out of the oven, and he'd immediately told her to apply some butter.

"I hope you're happy," she said as they loaded the last of the food onto the small hand cart that he'd brought with him and left outside the kitchen's back door. She'd hated every minute of scrubbing the pots and pans until they gleamed, even more than the cooking. He didn't blame her. Cleanup was no fun. But the biggest challenge still lay ahead.

"Where do you think you're going?" he asked when she turned to go back inside.

"I'm going to get changed, have a cool drink and get off my feet. Preferably someplace cool and shady."

TJ shook his head. "Not yet you're not."

She glanced down at herself in dismay. He knew what she was thinking. Her frock, so crisp and fresh this morning. was wilted, wrinkled, and stained with spills. Damp spots were visible under her arms. Her face was shiny, while her hair was a flyaway mess, her bonnet long ago abandoned. She had blisters on the tips of two of her fingers.

He almost felt sorry for her. "We've just gotten started."

Her eyes snapped at his, a challenge in their warm whisky depths. "I can hardly wait," she said, her words heavy with sarcasm.

"This way." He turned the cart in the direction of the road and started toward the station. Better he push it along the uneven roadway. In her hands, it would probably wind up flopped over sideways, the roadway a mess of spilled food.

"Any chance you might disclose our destination?" she asked icily.

"We'll be there soon enough."

With the festival packed up and the performers gone, the streets looked almost empty. If things had turned out different, him and Pa would have been part of the mass exit the other day. Instead, the little caravan was now parked under a large tree behind the warehouse.

Pa had made only a token protest at TJ's announcement they'd be staying put for a while. TJ had already sketched out a room in the loft of the warehouse that he planned to turn into living quarters first off. At least for himself. He suspected Pa would be more comfortable in familiar walls of

41

the old caravan. He was getting to an age where he didn't much care for change, convinced the old ways were best. TJ was still young enough and optimistic enough to believe better things lie ahead for anyone not afraid to take a chance.

Admittedly, many of his earlier risks had been a bust. Which didn't stop him from throwing his lot in with Chandra. He slid her a sideways look, wondering how it felt to set your sights on a goal like hers, hankering for the bright lights of some stage in a big Eastern city. TJ was happier in a town like Silver Springs Junction. Like Chandra's grandfather, he believed the town was on the cusp of being more than a junction for a handful of rail lines. Maybe for once, he'd be a part of the good life.

Chandra trudged along next to him, mercifully silent for a change. She needn't worry about running into anyone she knew. He doubted they'd even recognize her in her disheveled state.

"Are we headed for the warehouse?" she asked once they were close enough to smell the river.

"Nope." TJ kept going until they reached their destination. A hobo camp in the woods, beyond the town, but still close to the station. Every railway stop had them. Men who rode the rails across the country, usually in search of work. Markings on nearby posts or trees told the story of their findings in each location.

Symbols that meant nothing to the average person told the hobos if this was a safe place to camp, if work was available. The symbols warned if criminals or dangerous dogs were in the area, as well as places it was possible to get food in exchange for chores, and where the doctor could be found. It was an entire language that went right over the head of the average citizen.

As he expected, their arrival at the camp caused a stir. A few men rose to their feet, eyeing them warily, while others began to gather their scattered belongings, just in case.

"Over here," TJ said, low-voiced. He parked the hand truck and pulled Chandra to his side. "You take this smaller pot with the ladle. They won't view you as a threat."

"But—"

"They have their own plates."

Chandra huffed out a breath. "You expect me to serve them?"

"More than that," TJ said. "I expect you to do it graciously."

"I refuse," Chandra said haughtily. "I was not raised to serve people who are, who are—"

"Beneath you?" TJ sneered. "Just because they weren't born into wealth and good fortune doesn't make them less of people. They're proud. They don't like accepting charity. They want to work. They're also hungry. And smart enough to know they do better work with a full belly."

CHANDRA SET a stony glare at TJ as she picked up the smaller pot and ladle. She straightened and looked around. Remnants of blackened cooking fires dotted the area. Ragged bedrolls could be seen here and there, a respectful distance from others. Even in a place like this, folks prized their privacy.

And didn't appreciate the intrusion. That much was obvious from the dark, suspicious glances that came her way. The first man she approached turned away as if she wasn't there, his actions mimicked by the second man, as well as the third.

She sent TJ a hopeless shrug. Maybe now they could go back. It was dark here in the woods. Oppressive. Permeated by an air of hopelessness. Her shoulders slumped. It had been a long, exhausting day. And now it culminated in this? Homeless beggars who refused the food she had slaved over? How dare they!

To her surprise, one of the men rose and limped her way. His clothes were dirty, more rags than garments. He was barefoot. She tossed TJ a quick glance over her shoulder, even as she forced herself to stand her ground, ladle at the ready.

Instead of holding out his plate, the man took a small, rag-wrapped bundle from beneath his jacket and extended it her way.

"I found her by the tracks, alone and near dead," he said, his voice rusty as if from lack of use. "She needs milk and I don't got none."

The bundle of rags shifted to reveal a tiny newborn kitten, too weak to meow. It eyed Chandra with dull, milky eyes.

"Take her," the man said. "She at least deserves a chance."

Reluctantly, Chandra extended one hand. The kitten weighed next to nothing in her palm. "I don't think I can help her," Chandra said. "She's too young to be without her mother."

"Some creatures got no other choice."

His words hit her like a fist in her midsection. How old when she'd been orphaned? What would have happened to her and her sisters if Afi hadn't been on hand? To not only give them a home, but an education, a future.

She unwrapped the weak ball of fluff from the dirty piece of cloth and tucked it carefully into her skirt pocket, which was at least clean. "I'll take her to the animal doc," she said. "Provided you at least try my first attempt at cooking."

The man jerked his head in a tired nod and dug a metal plate and spoon from his misshapen pack. By the time Chandra dished up a ladleful of beans, TJ stood next to her breaking off a chunk of cornbread to add to the man's plate.

"Thank you," the man said, staring at his plate.

She'd never had a stranger thank her for being kind, and it was an unsettling feeling. But not an unpleasant one. Chandra looked around at the others. "Anyone else brave enough to try my cooking?"

It turned out they all were. In no time there was nothing left but a few empty pots and a pile of crumbs. As she watched this group of mismatched unfortunates shovel in the beans and cornbread, she felt something she'd never felt before. Along with exhaustion came a warm flicker of pride. She'd done this. Given these strangers a meal. Perhaps along with a full stomach, they also found a faint ray of hope. Their lives a little brighter.

She helped TJ reload the hand cart. By the time they were back into sunshine, her legs felt wobbly. She wished she could curl up on the wagon and have TJ drag her up the hill to the hotel. All she wanted was a hot bath and a soft bed. Luxuries unavailable to the men they'd just left.

"Have you been there before?" she asked.

"Not this one."

"You mean there are other places like that?"

He cocked her a mocking look. "Every place along the rail line where the train stops."

"But how? Why?"

"A lot of them came out here to help build the rail line. Once it was finished there was nothing for them to do."

"Can't they—Don't they have homes to go back to?"

"I expect most of them didn't have a home worth mentioning to start with."

Chandra was silent as they made their way up the hill. "Where are we going?" she asked when he turned down a side street.

"The vet's office."

She'd totally forgotten about the kitten. She rescued the tiny creature from her pocket and cupped it in her palm, praying it was still alive. Yes, she felt a faint heartbeat. Suddenly she was no longer tired. She cradled it to her bosom. Maybe the feel of her own heartbeat would encourage it to keep breathing. "We should hurry."

The animal doc frowned at the tiny scrap of fur she placed on his examination table. "Too young to be away from its mother."

"Surely there must be some way to give it a chance."

The vet gave her a beady-eyed look. "It'll cost ya."

She straightened. "Money is no object."

He huffed out a breath. "Leave her a few days and I'll see what I can do. She'll either make it or she won't."

She reached to stroke the soft head and was rewarded by a weak 'mew' and the faint flick of a tiny pink tongue against her hand. She beamed at the two men. "See? She's already stronger. She knows someone cares."

CHAPTER 6

"I can't believe my eyes!" Chandra marched into Afi's office and flung the week-old newspaper down onto the desk in front of him.

He gave it a disinterested glance. She'd bet her allowance he'd already seen it and gloated. "I have no control over what Douglas sees fit to print."

"I don't believe you. Someone fed that reporter fellow, Ryder Lyon," she sneered as she said his name, "a whole passel of information the ordinary person would have no knowledge of." She read aloud, stabbing the paper as she spoke. "Up and coming Silver Springs Junction welcomes new businessmen..... Land of opportunity. The way and the time is now. That's a direct quote from you."

"If it is?"

"And Bolton. Your lackey. Summoned here to do your bidding."

"You know there's no stopping your grandfather when he's mind's made up."

She gasped and spun to see Bolton rise lazily from behind a wingback chair near the fire. "Oh!" She didn't know if she ought to be angrier or apologetic. "Eavesdroppers rarely hear anything good said about themselves."

"It wasn't intentional. I was minding my own business, waiting for your grandfather to have a spare minute, when you burst in here like a typhoon."

She snatched up the paper and waved it toward him. "I bet you had something to do with this as well. It's practically a full-page advert inviting eligible bachelors here. It even mentions us—'...four accomplished and extremely personable granddaughters, one of whom is already spoken for.' We sound like a bunch of desperate old spinsters."

"Not you." Bolton shrugged. "I hear you've taken matters into your own hands. And who knows. Perhaps your sisters won't object to having a few interested suitors vying for their attention. Especially with you out of the running."

"You," Chandra leveled her attention on both men simultaneously. "Both of you are incorrigible."

"How's the theater coming along?" Bolton asked.

"None of your business." Chandra flounced from the room, slamming the door behind her.

Bolton looked over at Crawford. "Seems she doesn't approve the zeal with which you've approached finding the rest of them husbands."

"She'll wed that foppish clown or magician or whatever he calls himself over my dead body," Crawford said. "On top of which, I had nothing to do with the story Douglas ran."

"Sure, you didn't," Bolton said. "Sure, you didn't."

CHANDRA WATCHED the delivery men unload the first order of freshly milled lumber at the warehouse, barely able to stand still in excitement. Shakespeare, as she'd named the kitten, tried to wrap its small body around her ankles. She smiled down at the tiny scrap of fur. The animal doc had turned the kitten to her care as soon as it was able to lap milk from a saucer.

She'd been pleased the animal had survived, but a bit taken aback at this new responsibility. "What do I know about taking care of a cat?"

TJ had laughed at her. "They're independent creatures. Make her a bed in back of the theater, keep her saucer filled with milk and when she's big enough she'll help keep the mice under control."

And thus Shakespeare had become the theater watch cat, getting in the way of the workers and growing like a weed.

"Can you believe it, Shakespeare? It's really happening." These last weeks she had chafed with impatience as TJ spent what felt like forever taking measurements, sketching plans and drawing chalk marks on the floor before measuring some more. Just seeing the chalk marks, walking the perimeters of what would soon be a round center stage had been exciting, but the smell of freshly milled wood made the whole enterprise feel real.

"The lumber got here sooner than I expected."

Chandra laughed. "Silly. I told you Afi owns the mill. I simply told the foreman to make the order a priority."

TJ shook his head.

"What?"

"Just wondering how you'd fare if you didn't have everyone bending over backwards to do your bidding."

Chandra gave him a haughty look. "I learned from watching Afi. The fastest way to make things happen is to enlist the help of people who can assist you achieve your goals."

"I guess I fall into that category."

When she didn't refute his statement, he changed the subject. "What made you want to be an actress, anyway?"

Chandra pondered the question. What had sparked her interest?

"My sisters and I were really young. We'd just lost our parents and it was Christmas time. I guess Afi wanted to distract us. He took us to a Christmas play in whatever town we were in at the time. I'll never forget the magic of that night. The actors and actresses were like gods and goddesses. I wanted to be just like them when I grew up. I thought my mother must have wanted that too. Why else did she name me after a goddess?"

"The stage can be a hard life," TJ said.

"I like pretending to be someone else. I used to write short skits to act in with the children I was looking after. When I'm performing is when I feel like the real me." She frowned. "Isn't it that way for you, when you're on stage?"

TJ shook his head. "Nothing like it. We were always working or traveling to the next show. Ma trying to drum my lessons into me when she had the chance."

Chandra started. This was TJ's first mention of his mother, whom she assumed must have died young like hers had.

"What happened to her?" she asked softly.

He shrugged. "Ran off one day. 'S all I know. Pa took over my lessons. Sometimes we'd stick around one town or another for a while and he'd plunk me in school. I didn't like it much. Never fit in with the other kids."

"We moved all the time too," Chandra said, eager to find common ground. "We didn't like most of the governesses Afi hired. I guess we weren't very nice. None of them lasted long. Not until we came here. Miss Lester stayed with us for several years. I was sorry when she left."

"What happened to her?"

"It was really strange. One day she was here helping me write a play to perform for the hotel guests. Next day she was gone. No note or anything. Just gone. Afi didn't seem to know any more than we did. By that time the other girls were older and didn't really need a governess. Afi brought in a passel of different tutors to teach us all sorts of things. Whatever he figured we'd need to know, I guess."

～

DESPITE TJ'S PROTESTS, Chandra enlisted the skills of several tradesmen who had worked for Selene on the gaming hall.

"We can't afford to hire anyone," TJ grumbled.

"You let me worry about them getting paid," she said airily, ignoring TJ's glower. Didn't he see, the sooner the theater was in production, the closer to seeing their futures realized?

"Since when have you worried about a bill in your life?" boomed a voice from the back of the warehouse.

She started, then swung to face her grandfather. Since she hadn't heard him arrive, she resorted to girlhood exuberance, throwing herself into his arms as she had when she was younger. "Afi! Isn't it marvelous. TJ has the most insightful ideas. Like this center stage that people can view from anywhere inside, and this raised seating platform running along the walls. Every seat in the house will have a wonderful vantage point."

Afi gave her a brief hug and put her from him. "I thought I'd best come and see what all the fuss was about. I've heard from several disgruntled customers that their lumber order is behind schedule."

She pressed her lips together and lowered her gaze, standing with her hands behind her back as if she were a young child being chastised. "I learned a few tricks from watching you all these years. When you want something, don't let little hurdles get in the way."

"Perhaps you also need to learn, despite your enthusiasm, not to overstep. Isn't that right?" This last was directed at TJ who'd been silently watching the interaction between her and her grandfather.

"She does tend to be a bit of a tornado, not stopping to consider those who might get swept away in her path."

"Aren't you one to talk?" she fired back.

Afi held up his hands. "I didn't come here to incite a lover's quarrel." He turned to TJ. "Is your father comfortable staying out back?"

"He is. Thank you for allowing him to set up camp there. My room in the loft is nearly finished."

"You can't intend to live here in the theater once the two of you are married."

When she opened her mouth to speak, TJ shot her a warning look to stay silent.

"First things first. We can't make any plans until the theater is turning a profit so we can pay you back."

"Oh, but Afi won't—"

"This endeavor will not become a charity case. Your grandfather would lose all respect for me were I to become a kept man."

"Well said." Afi plopped his hat onto his head and turned to go. He paused to address TJ one more time. "I admit I was somewhat cynical when Chandra first broached this scheme of hers. I'm happy to see things progressing under your capable hand."

To her surprise, TJ sidled over and slid an arm around her shoulder. "She does tend to leap before she looks. I'm hoping it's an impulse she'll outgrow."

"Very good. Chandra, please arrange to have your young man to dinner one night. And his father of course. Your sisters and I are keen to get to know him better."

"Yes, Afi."

The second her grandfather was out of earshot, she shrugged off TJ's arm. "This is not good."

TJ's dark eyes fixed on hers. "What's not good?"

"You and your father to dinner. We can't let that happen."

"It's hardly an unreasonable request. Given that he thinks we are betrothed."

"He was supposed to leave me alone. Turn his attention to getting the others married off. After all, they're far older than me. Maia is minutes away from becoming an old maid."

"Are you worried I might embarrass you? Use the wrong fork?"

She blew out a breath. "I don't care about your table manners. I don't know the first thing about you. Which Afi will find peculiar, given that we are supposed to be forming a union."

"What would you like to know?"

"Any skeletons in the family closet?"

TJ laughed. "Every family has them. Even yours I'll warrant."

She stamped her foot impatiently. "This is hardly a laughing matter. We have to stay in Afi's good books. It's the only way."

"The only way for what?" drawled a different male voice from behind her.

Didn't anyone knock anymore? She whirled to face the newcomer. It was that pesky reporter Selene had kowtowed to in order to gain publicity for the gaming hall. She hoped she wouldn't have to play that game once the theater opened. "Mr. Lyon. I was under the impression that we'd seen the last of you."

"Funny thing about that." Ryder Lyon swept off his hat and advanced as he spoke. "I was on my way East, chatting to others on the train about the festival and the town itself, particularly your grandfather and how he got his start. It occurred to me there are still a lot of goings on below the surface. Rumors flying around that I had no chance to check out yet. First chance I had, I turned around and caught the next train back."

"How fortunate for us," she said sarcastically.

Lyon glanced around at the chaos of lumber, tools, and chalk marks on the floor. "Chasing in your sister's shadow?"

"I beg your pardon?"

"Selene has already made quite the name for herself with that gambling emporium. Met some folks on the train who were headed here for the express purpose of trying their luck."

She drew herself up as tall as she could. TJ stood to one side, arms crossed over his chest. She was grateful he didn't leap to her defense but allowed her to speak for herself.

"I'm extremely proud of Selene. Rest assured, her accomplishments have no bearing on what you see happening here."

Lyon gave her a long, searching look before turning to TJ. "I understand congratulations are in order. Trading up to an heiress is quite a coup for someone with your background." With that, Lyon tipped his hat and left.

She turned on TJ. "What did he mean by 'your background'?"

TJ shrugged. "He probably meant me being always on the move."

"I don't trust him," Chandra said darkly.

"Just don't alienate him. He might prove useful at some point."

No sooner had Lyon departed than the workers she'd hired arrived. The head carpenter conferred with TJ, the two men poring over plans spread out on a makeshift table fashioned from two sawhorses and a sheet of plywood while she chafed, miffed at being ignored. Wasn't this her project too?

Behind them, the other men began sorting through the stacks of lumber that had been delivered. She might as well have been invisible. She turned and made her way up the stairs that led to the upper loft. Perhaps one day they'd have extra seating up here, but for now they were concentrating on the main floor. A wall had been erected in the far corner, partitioning one section from the rest of the area. She rounded it and stopped.

Until he'd told Afi, she hadn't known TJ had set up temporary living quarters. She'd thought he was staying with his father in the caravan, but the evidence before her said otherwise. A mattress and a neat stack of bedding took up one side of the space. Clothing, including TJ's stage attire, hung from pegs nailed along one wall. She crossed the room to the window, which looked over the river. Through the copse of trees lay the temporary home for the hobos. How had TJ known it was there?

The caravan was parked out back not far from the river.

In front of it was a ring of stones and the blackened remnants of a cooking fire. What looked to be a wash line had been strung between two trees off to one side. Not far from the wash line was a hammock, sharing the trunk of one of the trees. The scene typified TJ's life to date, so different from hers. Even when they'd moved round the country, they'd always had a comfortable, furnished home and household help.

She spun about, only to walk directly into TJ behind her, all but bouncing off the hard wall of his chest.

"Admiring the view?" His hooded eyes gave away nothing.

She shouldn't feel defensive. After all, the entire property belonged to her grandfather. Yet, she had the strangest feeling that she had somehow impinged upon TJ's privacy. Trespassed in an area where she'd not been invited.

"I was just thinking about the difference in our backgrounds." She waved a hand toward the window.

"Is that all?"

It wasn't the first time she'd stood so close to him, but this time was different. The air between them suddenly felt thin. Her breathing accelerated. Waves of hot and cold rippled through her. Her skin tingled.

He stood taller than most men, making her feel tiny in comparison. His jaw was firm and square, shadowed by the beginnings of a day's whisker growth. His cheekbones were high and prominent, his cheeks hollowed beneath them. His lips were full. She wondered what they'd feel like atop hers.

Selene and Minerva had both been kissed. She'd heard them giggling about the way the men had seemed at a loss as to what to do with their hands. If Maia had ever been kissed, it was an experience her oldest sister elected not to share.

She had read about a man and woman kissing, of course. Somehow, she couldn't imagine that swoony feeling described in great detail in some of the romantic novels. Usually the couple were chaperoned, but occasionally managed to sneak away for stolen, breathless kisses.

Reading about the experience, she was happy to have been born in a time when a chaperone was no longer required to watch over a courting couple. Although she had been forced to duck from beneath her overprotective sisters' watchful eyes to see the festival. And TJ.

Her tongue slipped between suddenly dry lips. Her heart clamored so loudly she was sure it was audible to TJ.

"Be careful," he said. "Looking at a man like that can get a girl into trouble."

"Actually," she said boldly, "I was thinking it was time we kissed."

"Oh, were you now?"

"I mean—" She strove to keep her voice casual. "How are we supposed to act smitten around Afi and the others if we're virtually strangers?"

"Go ahead."

Her insides turned to mush as heated blood coursed through her veins. Carefully she rose up on tiptoe, placed her hands on his shoulders for balance, and tipped her head back. She still couldn't reach.

She smiled at the absurdness of the situation. "I think maybe you're supposed to help. Lower your head closer to mine or something."

"You think?" Amusement danced through his coal dark eyes. "You're not sure?"

"No doubt you've kissed more than your share of ladies,"

she said primly. "I, on the other hand, have lived a very sheltered life."

His hands clasped her firmly around her waist and
reeled her close to him. She felt like softened wax, melting
from his heat.

"Put your arms around my neck."

She did as he said, her fingers tangling in the wavy dark
hair that brushed the back collar of his shirt. As his lips
hovered above hers, she pressed her own lips tightly
together in anticipation.

The first brush of his lips on hers was disappointing.
What was the big deal? She pulled him closer, ground her
lips harder, felt his laughter against her mouth.

"You're not trying to roll out biscuits," he said. "Soften
your lips." His breath feathered over her and instinctively
she loosened her grip, sank bonelessly into him, lips parted.
That was better. His mouth moved teasingly over hers. Little
sips and gentle nibbles that sent ripples of pleasure up and
down her spine.

She felt the tip of his tongue outline the pliant seam of
her lips. When she parted her lips further, his tongue
slipped into her mouth as if it belonged there.

Liquid heat poured through her, setting her womanly
parts on fire. She shifted her hips against his, seeking more.
Boldly matching the exploration begun by him, she allowed
her tongue to dart into the heat of his mouth, to tangle
with his.

He groaned deep in the back of his throat and gathered
her close. His hands roamed her back, slid inside the neckline of her gown, his fingers cool against her overheated
skin.

She whimpered when he tore his mouth from hers. Only
to exhale in pleasure as he fastened his lips to the smooth

curve between shoulder and neck, eliciting the most delightful sensations, compounded by a gentle nip to the lobe of her ear. She shuddered when his tongue traced the inside curve of her ear, heat warring with his cool breath. He moved back to her mouth, plundered at length until she was quivering from head to toe before he finally put her from him.

"Do you think that might convince them we fancy each other?"

She felt as shocked as if he had dashed a spray of cold water in her face. How could he look so—so unmoved by what had just transpired?

She stepped back, amazed that her legs held her upright, refusing to let him see how his embrace had affected her. "Not bad for our first time," she said airily. "I dare say we might need a little more practice."

He laughed and turned to leave the room. "Anytime you like."

She watched him, fingers raised to her still-throbbing lips. It was all an act, she reminded herself. Practice makes perfect. Just like on stage.

CHAPTER 7

TJ whistled a familiar show tune as he left the warehouse and headed for the caravan. His father sat outside whittling, the way he did most days. Except the fire hadn't been lit. The washing line and hammock had both been taken down. The tune died on his lips. "What's going on?"

"We're leaving," his old man said.

"Hell we are. I'm just getting started here. Besides, we've been invited to the hotel for supper."

The old man spat onto the ground. "We don't belong there. With people like that."

"I heard you were the life of the party up there after the festival."

"That was different. I was the entertainment. I wasn't pretending to be one of them."

He gave his father a hard look. "Who's pretending?"

"Didn't you tell me you and that girl are pretending like you're betrothed?"

"That's different. Right now, the ruse suits both of us."

"Till it don't. Then you're out like yesterday's trash. We're simple people. Best you remember that."

TJ wasn't buying it. "You always taught me we're every bit as good as the next man."

His father gave him a dark look. "You crossed the wrong people before. I'd hoped you learned a thing or two. There are folks you just don't get involved with." He crooked his thumb up the hill in the direction of the hotel. "And those folks are some of 'em."

TJ's face tightened. "It wasn't like that and you know it."

"I know how it ended. Not about to sit around and witness that all over again."

"I've got a real chance here. To make a better life for both of us. To have a home for once. To quit moving around, putting on a show for drunks and idiots who think they're better than us."

His father heaved a weighty sigh. "Someone pays me off to leave town, I pay attention. Ain't no good to come from sticking around where you're not wanted. Those rich folks always get their way. Fair means or foul."

TJ's gaze narrowed. He didn't like the sounds of this. "You saying someone paid you to leave town. Who?"

"Don't rightly know. Found this shoved under the door. Don't know when or who."

His pa passed him a folded sheet of paper. The note inside was printed in crude block letter. 'A smart man knows when he's worn out his welcome. Your time here is up.'

"Had a stack of cash with it. No one needs to tell me a second time."

He stared down at the note. Crawford had seemed sincere the few times they'd spoken, but he had no doubt the man was used to having someone else do his dirty work. Maybe it was all an act. Maybe he didn't think TJ was good enough for his granddaughter. Or maybe his first instinct, not to trust any of the lot of them, had been right. Once he'd transformed the warehouse, Crawford and Chandra would take the place over, leaving him high and dry. If that was the case, it was a little soon to be getting rid of him. There was still a lot to do.

"You think this was meant for you or for me?"

"Who cares. We both go, they get what they want."

His mind raced. Was it possible he'd been seen lip-locked with Chandra? The sight rattling someone enough to try to send him packing?

"I'm not leaving," he said flatly.

His pa heaved a sigh. "I was a feared you might say that. Stubborn like your mother that way."

He tensed. Pa hadn't mentioned his ma since the day she disappeared from their lives. He took a closer look. "You're going to try and find her, aren't you?"

"You remind me so much of her, it's been kind of hard to forget. And now— now I'd like one more chance with her."

"She's the one who left."

"It wasn't all her fault," Pa said. "You're too young to remember. But I wasn't exactly easy to live with in the early days."

"Were you ever?" He tried to make it sound like a joke. Lighten things up.

"She wanted to stay put, just like you're trying to do. If I'm to stay put with one of you, I'd rather it was her."

He didn't know what to make of his pa's words. Memories of his mother were hazy. A head of thick black hair, dark eyes flashing with mischief. A way of moving that saw the men in the audience unable to tear their eyes from her. But it was only a child's perception. Could also be something he'd imagined to help get over the pain of being abandoned.

"What kind of mother leaves her child behind?" he said bitterly.

"It weren't like that. She wanted you with her. I—I wasn't very nice about it. I couldn't do the act on my own."

"If that's the case, what makes you think she'll take you back?"

"I won't rest easy till I try." His pa pointed to the note and the money. "Kind of felt my decision was made for me. You sure you won't come?"

He recalled Chandra's untried lips beneath his. He wasn't one to get his head turned by a woman's attention. Not these days. But he'd made a deal and he intended to see it through. Not only that, he needed to find out who wanted him out of town. If someone had it out for him, best he know that, too.

"Sounds like something you need to do on your own."

"Could be you're right."

He watched his father harness their tired old horses. The pair sent him an imploring look, as if to say, 'Really? We like it here'. He only hoped they got his Pa to his destination.

"Do you even know where she is?"

"Got a fair idea."

His pa wasn't given to displays of emotion, so the suspicious shine in the old man's eyes as he said good-bye made him call out. "Wait."

Pa turned to him.

"I'll miss you."

"Me too," his pa said as he gathered up the reins. "You watch your back."

"You too."

He followed him to the road and watched till the caravan was out of sight. He was still staring into the distance when Chandra appeared at his side.

"Whatcha looking at?"

He started. "Nothing. Place looks different with the festival gone. That's all."

"Speaking of gone, I noticed the caravan's not in its usual place."

Nothing got by her. "Pa decided Silver Springs Junction wasn't for him after all."

She looked at him with eyes that saw too much. Or tried to. Sometimes he had the sense of her peeling back his skin, layer by layer. Which wasn't possible. He'd thickened his skin to rival the hide of a buffalo. Prison had taught him that.

"In that case I'd better go tell Cook to expect one less for the evening meal."

He watched her stride back up the street. It still looked naked to him without the tents and crowds and performers. Not that she didn't pass other folks along her way, pausing now and again to talk to them. The true lady of the manor.

How different it must feel to belong someplace. Know who you were from the outset and accept it as your due. He'd grown up being someone else. Someone his folks expected him to be, a child prodigy in a magician's hat. Which eventually morphed into being the person spectators expected to see up there on the stage.

He was older before he figured out how much the patrons enjoyed being shocked and surprised when he didn't always act according to their expectations. And he could shock with the best of them, turn the tables so fast that those watching had no idea what just happened.

Still, he needed to figure out who he really was. Maybe that was the purpose of his stay in Silver Springs Junction.

~

AFTER INFORMING Cook to expect one less for dinner, Chandra passed Afi's study on the way to the stairs. The door was slightly ajar, the male voices coming from inside clear enough to make her stop and listen. While their voices rose and fell, the thrust of the conversation was clear. Shock and anger surged through her in waves.

The conversation's abrupt end was followed by scrape of chair legs against the wooden floor. Quickly she ducked out of sight and took the back stairs to her room, her mind racing and her heart pounding. No way would they get away with this!

That evening, she took extra care with her appearance. After all, she was supposed to be betrothed, excited to introduce her intended to friends and family before the evening meal. She needed to look the part of the blushing bride-to-be, and was almost ready when Maia came flying through the door, gasping for breath as if she'd just run up the stairs.

"Mercy, the time does get away," Maia said as she peeled out of her work gown in one motion before splashing water on her flushed cheeks and smoothing her hair with damp hands. "Beckett is already downstairs with Selene. I didn't know they planned to join us. Usually they're at the Emporium."

"I believe Afi called for the entire family to be here." At least, that was her impression, given what she'd overheard.

"Do you think—Is it possible Afi is planning to spring any surprise guests on us this evening?"

"You know Afi," Chandra said with forced casualness as she studied her reflection in the looking glass. "Always full of surprises."

Tonight, he was about to get a surprise of his own. "See you down there."

"Chandra?"

She turned.

"Are you quite sure about your betrothal? You know so little about this man."

Her eyes narrowed. "What have you heard?"

"No—nothing," Maia said.

"Afi gave us his blessing."

"True. I just— I only want you to be happy."

"Trust me when I say I know exactly what I'm doing."

Or so she hoped.

She was taken aback to find TJ waiting for her at the bottom of the stairs. "I thought you'd be with the others." Snippets of conversation and laughter spilled through the open doorway of the parlor.

"I thought it best we present a united front." He looped his arm at his side so she could tuck her hand through. "Wait. I almost forgot." He released her and pulled a small velvet pouch from his pocket, spilling a half dozen rings into his palm. Gemstones winked up at her in the light from the nearby lamp. "One of these ought to fit. See anything you like?"

She sucked in her breath. "Are they stolen?"

His eyes hardened. "I might be a lot of things. But I'm no thief. From time to time Pa would be approached by a wealthy wife, eager to learn a few magic tricks. If they didn't want their husbands to know how they acquired their newfound skills, this was how they paid him."

"In that case." She fingered the offerings. "I was always partial to emeralds."

"The emerald it is." He took her left hand and slipped the ring onto her fourth finger. "Good fit."

"Rest assured I'll see you get it back. Meanwhile, I'll take these others." She plucked the velvet bag from his fist. "Maia can put them into the hotel safe. You shouldn't leave valuables lying around in the warehouse with all those workers coming and going. It's not common knowledge, but thieves have been busy in the town, relieving wealthy patrons of their baubles."

He laughed. "No one would expect a lowly magician to own anything of value."

"Have you or your father never tried to sell them? I'm sure the money would be useful."

"Pa and I always had enough. Besides, he wasn't convinced folks would believe he got them fair and square."

"I see," she said. "Why didn't he refuse payment if he didn't need the money?"

"Pa believes rich folks have little or no appreciation for things that don't cost them. If he gave away his secrets for free, they'd have no meaning."

"So, anything worth having is worth paying for."

"The higher the price, the greater the perceived value."

"What does that say about your involvement in our warehouse project?"

His lips curled cynically. "On the surface, I'm paying the ultimate price. My freedom. Not to mention that at any minute it could all be taken away should your grandfather decide he wants the building back."

TJ was right. Afi could be fickle. Turning the warehouse into a theater was her means to get out of town and strike out on her own. Unlike TJ, who'd been on his own forever and saw it as a means to stay put.

"Tell me. How did you convince your grandfather to fund the improvements?"

"Simple. I told him if he didn't put up the funds, I'd secure them from one of his rivals."

Before he could comment, there was a sound of footsteps on the stairs. Seconds later, Maia was at their side.

Her sister looked from one to the other. "What are you doing out here?"

"Waiting for you." She passed Maia the velvet pouch. "Can you please put this into the safe for TJ?"

"Right away. You'd better go in. Isn't this your night?"

It most certainly would be.

CHAPTER 8

B efore Chandra made her appearance at the top of the stairs, TJ had been puzzling over where he'd seen the older woman he'd glimpsed hurrying from the hotel when he arrived. It hadn't been here in town, but memory eluded him as to where. A mystery soon forgotten as Chandra selected which ring to wear for appearances sake. He'd been taken aback when she insisted the others be stored in the hotel safe. He couldn't recall a woman ever expressing concern on his behalf. Well, only once. Under entirely different circumstances.

The minute she ushered him into the parlor, he felt like he was back on stage. He shook hands with Crawford, resisting the impulse to scrape and bow before he was introduced to the other folks gathered. Chandra's sisters he'd seen with her at the festival.

Some of the other guests looked familiar as well. Beckett. Bolton. He'd always been good at remembering names, and took his time as he was introduced around the room.

After which there was a lull. The others appeared to be watching him, signaling his cue to speak. "I'd like to thank you, Mr. Crawford for your hospitality. And for readily accepting me here. With that in mind, sir, I brought you a small token of thanks."

From his jacket pocket he produced a plain black fountain pen and presented it to the older man, who frowned as he accepted it. He smiled as Crawford studied the writing implement, aware of what his host was no doubt thinking. That he already owned much fancier pens. He waited for Crawford to meet his gaze.

"It might not look like much, but I think you'll find it has its uses."

"How's that?" Crawford asked.

"Simple." TJ pulled a folded sheet of paper from his pocket. "If you could sign your signature."

"What is it? A bank draft payable to you?"

The guests laughed awkwardly, as if not quite sure what to make of a lowly magician from the wrong side of the tracks, taking up with the youngest Crawford heir.

Luckily, he'd worked tougher crowds than this. "I assure you. It's blank," he said in his best on-stage voice.

Crawford moved to the piano, unfolded and smoothed the paper before signing his name with a flourish. He held up the paper for the guests to see. "Works fine," he said. "Very nice nib."

"Just wait," TJ said, aware of Chandra shifting from foot to foot next to him.

"May I please have the paper back, sir?"

Crawford handed it over.

In his best theatrical fashion, TJ folded the paper in half, waved it through the air a few times, then unfolded it and displayed it to the guests. He heard the indrawn gasp of amazement. The page was blank. He showed both sides to make his point.

"What did you just do?" Crawford blustered.

"Me? Not a thing. It was all you. The pen in your hand contains a special ink which becomes invisible a short time later."

Chandra broke into applause, quickly joined by those watching. He gave the crowd a cynical once over. Did they expect him to bow and leave the room.

"Thank you, young man. I shall be sure to use it judiciously."

"About that," Chandra said, her words tumbling over themselves in an effort to be heard. "When were you and Bolton planning to disclose what I heard you discussing earlier? Were you saving it for the dinner table? Or intending to keep to yourselves your discovery that TJ spent time in jail? I mean, it's hardly fair to talk about it behind his back without giving him the opportunity to tell his side."

You could have heard a pin drop. He didn't know if he should applaud Chandra for her over-the-prow attack, or put her over his knee for not warning him. Now he understood her concern for the jewelry he'd had on his person. Full points for the subtle way she'd relieved him of it. Not that he expected anyone here would ask him to empty his pockets but—

And so typical not to warn him. Almost as if she knew he'd been declared wrongly convicted and released. He eyed the other guests. Would they even believe him if he professed his innocence?

When no one said a word, Chandra continued. "Let he who is above reproach cast the first stone."

"That most certainly will not be me. Nor should it be you, Crawford." TJ, along with everyone else, turned toward the speaker. Chandra's sister Maia had noticeably paled.

The speaker, obviously newly-arrived, entered the room with a jovial smile.

"Mr. Douglas," Maia said stiffly. "I was given to understand you had checked out of the hotel."

"True enough, Miss Crawford. But Silver Springs Junction has quite grown on me during my short stay. Your grandfather was kind enough to rent me one of the new houses he's had built."

Angling his gaze between Crawford and Douglas, TJ sensed a thinly-veiled antagonism between the two men.

"A deal he cemented with a kind offer to dine with the family this evening. I do apologize for my tardiness. It appears I missed a fair bit of drama."

"The girls are forever finding new ways to be dramatic," Crawford said. "I see poor Flo wringing her hands in the doorway, which means supper is about to grow cold if we don't all move to the dining room."

TJ followed Chandra to the dining room. Did no one care why he'd spent time behind bars? Or were they too polite to say anything? The rich definitely were different.

CHANDRA PUSHED her food around on her plate. Individual conversations flowed over her from all sides, while the bomb she dropped before dinner might as well not have happened. Worse yet, it didn't appear TJ would get the chance to tell his side. Was she the only one who cared enough to want to know why he'd been in jail? Or how long since he'd been released?

She tried to catch his eye. Send a silent apology for not telling him what she was about to do, counting instead on the element of surprise for him to spill the whole story.

Except he refused to meet her gaze, focusing instead on a subdued conversation with Beckett on his other side.

Talk of the recent influx of newcomers to their humble town following the success of the festival dominated the table. Cynically, she wondered if any of the recently-imported men were earmarked for Minerva or Maia. Lord help her sisters. Or worse yet her, before taking matters into her own hands with her fake betrothal to TJ. For the first time in her life, she was on track to getting what she wanted. A way out.

As the meal ended, TJ rose and pulled out her chair, his voice low in her ear as the group moved en masse to the parlor for after dinner drinks. "Whatever you hoped to prove didn't pan out."

She tugged his sleeve, pulling him aside to a corner of the lobby, away from prying eyes. "I don't like it when people talk behind someone's back."

He gave her an enigmatic look. "It's been happening my entire life."

"Why were you in jail?"

"None of your concern."

"Of course it concerns me. For all intents and purposes, you and I are betrothed."

He leaned in so close she could feel the heat of his breath. His eyes were the black of gathering thunderstorms, his mouth tight with emotion. "Make no mistake, Chandra. Were you really my woman, things between us would be a whole lot different."

Her heart pounded with excitement at the way he emphasized 'my woman'. For one mad, impulsive second, she wished it were so. That she really was his woman. That he would pull her to him. Mark his territory. Brand her his. As she swayed toward him, his strong hands gripped her upper arms, preventing her from brushing against him. Instead, he put her from him, turned and strode into the parlor.

She took a second, fanning herself with her hand in an attempt to bring her color back to normal. Then she sailed regally into the parlor as if nothing had happened, standing in what she judged to be a safe place next to Selene and Beckett.

"How are things at the Emporium?" she asked, a trifle miffed that no one had asked a single question this evening about the progress on the theater.

"Finally calming down, now that the festival is over," Selene said. "Exactly the way Beckett predicted it would." She sent a loving look his way. A look he returned in such a way Chandra's stomach twisted itself into a knot. Not that she wished a certain magician would look at her that same way.

"It's no longer necessary to spend every waking moment in the place," Beckett said, slowly trailing one hand the length of Selene's bare arm. "We can enjoy some time together, just the two of us."

"And plan the wedding," Selene said. "Afi insists on it being the social event of the season, which seems a lot on the heels of the festival."

"As I keep reminding you, my dear. It is our special day. Your grandfather need not always have everything his way."

Selene laughed. "Try telling that to him."

With a murmured excuse Chandra helped herself to a cup of coffee and drifted toward where Minerva and Maia sat stiffly on a settee, hands tucked between their knees. The two looked as if their faces were carved from stone.

Minerva tugged her down to their level so abruptly

some of her coffee sloshed into the saucer. "Did you know that TJ had been in jail?" she whispered.

"Of course not," she whispered back, straightening before the rest of her coffee ended up in the saucer.

"Ohhhh," Minerva said as Chandra picked up her cup. "Is that ring from TJ?"

"As a matter of fact, it is." Chandra extended her hand toward both her sisters, admiring the shape of the bauble on her finger and the way the gaslight lit up the tiny diamonds ringing the emerald.

Lila must have caught the gesture for she drifted their way. "I hear congratulations are in order," she said. "Has any date been set?"

Chandra shifted uncomfortably. When they were young, her sisters had an uncanny way of knowing when she wasn't telling the truth. She hadn't had occasion lately to test their powers. "We're holding off until after Selene and Beckett tie the knot. Get to know each other better." She smiled guilelessly at her sisters. "Perhaps by that time you two will be planning weddings of your own."

Deflecting further unwanted questions from her sisters, she turned to Lila. "And congratulations to you."

Lila flushed. "How did you—?"

"Your book being published? It's common knowledge. I just haven't seen you to wish you well."

"Oh, that," Lila said breezily. "I turned down their offer."

"Oh." Now Chandra felt foolish. She'd been so wrapped up in her own affairs she'd not kept up with happenings around town.

"They wanted me to use a man's first name. Or at best, only initials. Bolton convinced me to look elsewhere. He said if one publisher is interested in publishing the book, surely others will be as well."

"Do you have the services of a literary agent, my dear?" Callan Douglas slid effortlessly into their conversation as if he'd been there the entire time. "Because I'd be happy to offer introductions to a few in my acquaintance."

"That would be wonderful, Mr. Douglas. Thank you. I may take you up on that."

"Callan, please. Anytime. Whatever I can do to help." He turned his attention Maia's way. "I've been curious to know what became of the tunnels below the hotel?"

"Afi is supposed to be having them sealed off," Maia said. "It was a bit of fancifulness on his part, having them in the first place."

"Cagey fellow your grandfather. I'd keep an eye on him if I was you."

"Same to be said for you, Callan." Afi joined them and turned to Lila. "Whatever this chap says, make sure you get it in writing."

"Fine," Callan quipped. "Mind if I borrow that new pen you received earlier?"

While the two men laughed uproariously, Chandra cast a glance toward TJ, who stood off to one side in what appeared to be a heated conversation with Bolton. Was Bolton asking him about his time in jail? Maybe her bold statement had the desired effect after all, and give TJ the chance to tell his side. Something she desperately wanted to hear for herself.

"Chandra." She flinched at the tone of Afi's voice. She'd heard that tone before, but never directed toward her. It was his deep, formidable, 'you've stepped over the line and I'm going to make you sorry' voice she'd heard directed at wayward workers and unfortunate members of his staff over the years.

"Yes, Afi," she said sweetly, looking around the room for

help, but everyone else appeared embroiled in their own conversations. No one was paying the two of them any mind.

"Your remark earlier was most uncalled for. Neither ladylike, nor suitable supper hour conversation. You've disappointed me greatly."

Chandra lowered her gaze. She was not sorry in the least, but perhaps if she acted penitent Afi's ill will would blow over.

"You're of an age, which makes it pointless for me to forbid any association with acquaintances of a questionable background. But I'm nobody's fool. I did not make my fortune by investing with known criminals."

Chandra gasped. Afi withdrawing his financial support was a blow she had not anticipated.

"You don't know TJ committed a criminal act."

"Apparently a court of law was convinced of his duplicity. Enough to render a sentence for his wrongdoings."

"You're not even going to hear his side?" She struggled to keep her voice down, so as to not call attention to their conversation.

"The young man's side of things matters naught. The fact that he was convicted of a crime is enough for me."

Chandra frowned. "I never knew you to be so close-minded."

"Caution is a trait that comes with age and experience. One I hope you learn to embrace one day in the not-too-distant future. The others always maintained I coddled you, what with you being the youngest."

"Pish, tish and nonsense," Chandra said. "You raised us all equally."

It seemed they were not being as quiet as Chandra thought. Or else TJ sensed discord simply from her stance as she faced her grandfather. Either way he appeared at her side, his arm comforting around her midsection.

"Your grandfather is right, Chandra. Your reputation will be harmed should word spread about my past. Any joint endeavors are doomed to failure. Bolton, acting as your grandfather's agent, has promised none of this will be discussed if I just disappear."

"And thereby effectively ending our betrothal. Well, I won't hear of it." Chandra crossed her arms over her chest and moved closer to TJ. "Afi is not the only one in town with means. We will find another way to complete the warehouse's transformation."

Afi stiffened. "Don't forget who owns the property."

Fury and disappointment surged through her veins. "You signed a long-term lease agreement. One which I doubt you would risk the ensuing scandal were you to try and break it. You have plans for this town. Well so do we."

Afi gave her a hard look. "You would go against your family? Side with an outsider of questionable background."

She clung to TJ. "I am prepared to fight for what I believe is right. A lesson learned on your knee at a very early age."

Afi hunched slightly, then straightened. "You do not have my blessing. Which means you're on your own. Best of luck to you."

Chandra slumped, feeling as if the stuffing had been knocked out of her. She had never been on the receiving end of Afi's anger or disapproval, let alone defied him. She'd simply worked him around so she got her own way. Now, however, she longed to be on her own and out from under his thumb. She'd heard it said one needed to let certain things go in order to gain others of far more importance.

TJ watched her, concern in his eyes. "Are you sure about

this? It's not too late to set things right with him if I fade from the picture."

She squared her shoulders. "You and I have a deal. You're not going anywhere." Then she marched from the room, head high.

In the kitchen, she opened the door of the refrigerator's cold box and began pulling out bowls of food leftover from their evening meal. So Afi was cutting her off, was he? Did that mean he was banishing her from her living quarters here at the hotel as well? Somehow, she doubted it.

She piled scoops of leftover ham and chicken onto a metal serving platter. Having never wanted for a thing, she'd not given any thought to those with less. Seeing the camp by the river had been eye-opening. How did TJ even know it was there? Perhaps at some point he'd been beholden on the charity of others for his next meal or lodging. Maybe after he'd been in jail.

She knew so little about him.

She longed to know more. Longed to know everything.

CHAPTER 9

TJ watched Chandra leave the room. She wasn't the first woman to walk away from him, starting with his mother. After he reached an age where he discovered women were drawn to his looks, he took full advantage. Always careful to make certain he was the one doing the leaving.

The one time he'd gone against his pattern had proven his undoing, and he wasn't about to make that mistake again.

Unsure of his standing with the remaining guests, he drifted from conversation to conversation, always on the outskirts. He might as well have been invisible. Chandra did not return, and he was preparing to slip away when he was cornered by the latecomer to dinner, Callan Douglas.

"I've been watching you," the other man said.

"So?" TJ's hands fisted reflexively. He'd hoped his days of having to prove his worth were a thing of the past, but if tonight was any indication—

"I admire your foresight. Turning an unused warehouse into an entertainment hub. With limitless possibilities. I had a snoop inside one evening and was impressed by the innovative design."

TJ swallowed thickly. One evening. Did that mean that while he was asleep upstairs this man had been creeping through the main floor? "Do you make a habit of trespassing?" he asked lightly.

Callan shrugged. "Chalk it up to curiosity. No malicious intent involved. Besides, the owner and I go back aways. Seemed unlikely there'd be charges coming from that quarter."

"Next time you're in the mood for a tour, ask first," TJ said brusquely.

Callan threw back his head and laughed. "I'm in the first house on Madeira Lane, if you happen to be looking for me. I'm pretty sure we can help each other out. Bring Crawford's granddaughter. Speaking of Chandra, just before you and I started our little chat I saw her trudging down the hill toward town. You might want to go after her. Gal has a habit of leaping before she looks. I'm pretty sure she's responsible for most of Crawford's gray hair."

"You waited till now to tell me?" TJ spun on his heel without so much as a by-your-leave to the others, tore from the room and took off down the hill. Blast the woman. Was she intent on burning every bridge and tossing herself atop the blaze? Didn't she know better than be out this late on her own?

He reached the station without catching sight of her and was standing about feeling useless when his eye caught a fleeting blur of movement heading toward the river. He caught up with her as she approached the hobo camp.

"Oh good." She turned and thrust a heaped serving platter into his arms. "This is getting heavy."

The platter was covered with a kitchen cloth, but the

enticing smell of cooked food wafted from beneath it. He heard a plaintive meow and looked down to see the theater kitten, Shakespeare she'd named him, looking up at him.

"What's the cat doing here?"

"She followed me from the theater. I thought her rescuer might enjoy seeing how well she's doing."

He shot her a suspicious look. "What are you—?"

"The men were gracious enough before, to eat my attempt at cooking. Think how much they'll enjoy a well-prepared meal."

"You raided the hotel kitchen?"

"I did. It's hardly fair we have so much while others have so little. I thought I'd even the score a little."

The dusk gave up a scuffling sound around them as a few hobos crept forward to see what was going on. Chandra lifted a corner of the kitchen towel, picked up a heavy serving fork and banged the edge of the platter. "Gentlemen. Dinner is served."

Tentatively at first, then growing bolder, the men approached, tin plates extended. Chandra mounded mashed potatoes and a slab of meat onto each one. A few spoke but most merely acknowledged her with a grunt of thanks. Several stooped to give Shakespeare a scratch behind her ears, including the man who had first rescued the kitten. His time-worn face creased in a rusty smile as he was rewarded with a loud humming purr.

Chandra smiled. "She remembers you."

He stiffened and shuffled away quickly, as if embarrassed to be singled out.

"He doesn't talk much," TJ said, holding the platter steady as Chandra finished dispersing the food. Once done, she folded up the cloth, and looked over at him.

"Shall we?"

He nodded and followed as she scrambled up the river bank, Shakespeare at her heels. "Aren't you worried what your grandfather will say when he finds the larder empty?"

She shrugged. "He's already voiced his displeasure with me. I might as well do something to warrant it."

When they reached the street, Shakespeare ran off toward the theater while TJ grabbed her hand and spun her to face him. "You should walk away," he said gruffly. "From the warehouse project and from me."

"Apparently you don't know me very well, Mr. Dirks."

He worked to keep a straight face. No one ever called him Mr. Dirks, let alone sounded so righteous saying it.

"Nothing good comes from women who associate themselves with me."

"Why don't you explain that statement?"

"It's a long story."

"I have all night." Reaching the station, she plunked herself onto a nearby bench. Moonlight shone on the engraved brass plaque stating the bench had been a gift to the town from Benjamin Crawford; the irony not lost on him. Her grandfather owned this town, along with everything and everyone in it. Chandra would never break free.

"I assume you'd like to know what I did to land in jail?"

Chandra sniffed. "Sounds to me like a woman was involved."

"Very astute." What had happened to the immature and unworldly girl he'd met a short time ago? Somehow, when he wasn't looking, she had turned into a benefactress who rescued an abandoned kitten, fed those down on their luck, and openly defied her grandfather. Now she was intuiting things about him without being told.

"My father continues to pine for my mother, even

though she left him. Left us. I determined to never suffer the same fate."

"By amusing yourself with a selection of women as you travel the country."

He shrugged. "We managed to amuse each other for a short time. The rules were clearly understood. No attachments."

"Someone broke those rules," she guessed.

"Someone who should have known better. Me." He shifted to face her. He'd never been so honest with another person. Never felt the need before now. "I did not know she was married; her husband out of town. I started to think—" He blew out a breath. "It doesn't matter. One night while we were together, her husband, who had found out about us from others, planted the contents of her jewelry box in my rucksack back at the caravan. He waited until we parted, then called the sheriff."

"And you wound up in jail."

"Where I'd still be if not for the wife. I don't know her motivation, but she told the judge she'd been planning to leave her husband. She claimed I was simply a friend she'd entrusted her valuables to. The judge didn't like it, but she must have been convincing. Enough that he reversed his ruling and I was set free."

Chandra's eyes on his were wide. "Did you ever see the woman again?"

"She and her husband left town. Meanwhile, my father had moved on. I knew he always followed the road closest to the railway line." He waved a hand back the way they'd come. "For a while, I was one of those men you saw tonight."

"Until you caught up with your father."

He nodded. "He acted as if I'd never been gone. We

never spoke about what happened. But I learned the lesson well. Never trust a woman."

"Even though a woman helped secure your release?"

"It was because I trusted her that I ended up branded as a criminal. A fact which follows me to this day."

Chandra lowered her eyes to her lap. "No wonder you resent me for tricking you into acting the role of my betrothed."

"I still don't understand the reasoning behind it."

"Have you ever felt trapped?"

He laughed humorlessly. "I spend my life in a caravan, amusing people I care nothing about. Performing magic stunts that bore me. You just heard my story of being wrongfully jailed."

She nodded. "The cage might be gilded, but I feel every bit as trapped. Treated well, but patted on the head and never taken seriously. On top of which, Afi has made it his life's mission to see my sisters and I all married off within the next year."

He whistled softly. Desperate situations led to desperate acts. "Do all your sisters feel the same way? Trapped in their lives?"

"Selene might have once. But now she has not only the emporium, she has Beckett as well. Maia has the hotel. Minerva distracts herself with her art." She waved one hand through the air. "Look around you. There is no opportunity here for me to earn any sort of notice as a credible actress."

He sat back. She'd used him, as had many women before her. This time felt different. He'd make it different.

He stood and pulled her to her feet. She was beautiful in the moonlight, her eyes wide, her expression purposeful as she gazed up at him. Maybe they weren't so different from each other, after all.

"How well do you know Callan Douglas?"

She wrinkled her nose. "Why?"

"I sense an underlying animosity between him and your grandfather."

"I believe it's more of a friendly competition. Afi feels Callan has too much political influence. He can't afford the man as an enemy, but he doesn't trust him as a friend."

He nodded. "That explains a lot."

Chandra had not moved from the loose circle of his arms. In fact, she had edged even closer as they spoke, gently reaching up to smooth a strand of hair from his forehead. Her eyes on his were soft, her lips curved in a half smile. "I sense an idea looming."

"Earlier this evening, Douglas told me to come see him. And to bring you along."

Chandra flung her arms around his waist and hugged him tight. "Do you know what this means?"

He was too distracted by her body pressed snugly against his to answer.

She leaned back, arms linked behind his back, and raised her face to his. "It means we have ourselves a silent partner. Callan has the means to fund the theater. And he'd enjoy nothing more than a one-up on Afi."

He lowered his head toward hers. Perhaps he wasn't as different from other men as he thought, easily bewitched by the temptation of a soft female body in his arms. When his lips found hers, all other thought disappeared. Nothing existed save him and her, together in the moonlight.

She parted her lips eagerly, clearly remembering what he had taught her last time. Shyly at first, her tongue teased his. The result was far sweeter, far more intoxicating than if she'd been well schooled in the art of kissing.

Her hands moved from his middle to slide sensuously

up his back, probing tense muscles as he held her wrapped against him. Her hips swayed against his with an instinct as old as time, and it was all he could do not to grind himself against her. Cool fingers grazed the back of his neck seconds before her fingers ploughed through his hair.

She trembled. Her breath caught in anticipation as he ripped his lips from hers and trailed a light, teasing trail of kisses down her throat. She sighed and tilted her head, granting him further access. Access to plant a series of moist, open-mouthed caresses against the soft swell of skin exposed above the neckline of her gown. He longed to bury his face into the welcoming V of her bosom. To nuzzle down, finding and fondling the turgid tips of her breasts with his tongue. To feel the soft peaks beneath his fingertips as he molded and remolded their shape, his callused palms scraping her aroused nipples until she sobbed with need.

He'd kiss his way past her belly down to that hidden treasure trove between her legs to find her damp with need. Her breath rising and falling in shallow pants as he—

Her hands gripped his head, forcing his mouth back to hers. She was innocent, he reminded himself. With no idea of what ultimately transpired between a man and a woman.

He kissed her softly, swallowing his regret that he would not be the one to educate her in the ways a man and woman bring each other pleasure. He stood, breathing heavily, his forehead resting against hers as his blood cooled and he was able to pick up their conversation.

"Why would Callan be after a foothold in this town? I mean there are plenty of towns in the West that he could take over and call his own."

Her hands still encircled his forearms as if she was loathe to release him. "Friendly rivalry with Afi, most likely."

Friendly? Or not so friendly?

The town clock chimed midnight. Where had the hours gone?

"Come. I'd best get you home before your grandfather adds kidnapping and food theft to my list of crimes."

CHANDRA HAD NEVER FELT OSTRACIZED before; secretly believing she was Afi's favorite. But when he continued to convey his displeasure by ignoring her, she dug in her heels and ignored him back. She remained absent from family meals and continued to raid the hotel larder to take food to the men living in the hobo camp. Before long she began practicing some of her stage personalities and gestures around them, gratified when they didn't take their food and scurry off, but settled in to watch her antics.

They were a nonjudgmental audience, and their unexpected applause one night was music to her ears. This is what she was meant to be doing. Not here in the dusky shadows of a river camp, but on stage with lighting and sound before a sophisticated audience.

Callan Douglas had willingly stepped in as a silent partner for the theater, and with his contacts the work was progressing at a steady clip. Every time she stopped in, she got a better sense of what the finished product would look like. And she couldn't wait.

She was in the kitchen late one evening, washing the empty platter she'd taken to the river camp, when she looked up to see Maia behind her, wearing a disapproving frown.

"I don't know what you're up to Chandra, but it needs to stop and it needs to stop now."

She flicked the drying cloth against the platter, then stacked it on the shelf with the others.

"I don't know what you mean."

"You're never here. You creep around the hotel at night when you think we're all asleep. On top of which Cook has noticed food missing on a regular basis."

"I get hungry," she said.

"Significant amounts of food missing," Maia said. "Enough, as Cook put it, to feed a small army. I haven't said anything to Afi. Yet. Things are strained enough between you two." She pulled up a chair and collapsed into it as if her body suddenly felt too heavy for her legs to support it. Her expression was nothing but kind. "You and I always used to be able to talk to each other, remember? No matter what was going on with the others. I hate that things suddenly feel different."

Chandra hung the drying towel on the line above the stove and pulled a second chair close to her sister. "Things *are* different. We're no longer children. Selene is planning her wedding. The hotel has never been so busy. I'm doing what I can to help TJ with the warehouse alterations—"

"You're going ahead with that? Without Afi's blessing."

"Afi's not the only man to wield any influence around here."

Maia's face paled. "Callan Douglas. Chandra you mustn't. Afi will never forgive you when he finds out."

Chandra rose. "You're being dramatic. Douglas is a regular guest at Afi's table."

"For which I'm certain Afi has his reasons." Maia grabbed her hand and stared hard at the ring from TJ. "You know this is most likely stolen."

She snatched her hand back. "You have no right to make that judgement."

"Don't I? I'd be extremely interested to hear how he came to have that cache of jewels you had me tuck into the safe for him."

Chandra blanched. "You also had no right to snoop through TJ's property."

"My hotel. My safe. I have every right."

"I think you're forgetting. It's Afi's hotel."

"And we are his family."

She sat back down, slowly this time. "How will you feel when he introduces you to a man he intends to marry you off to? A perfect stranger. Will you sit still for that? Because I've already decided I'm not having any of it."

She watched as realization dawned across Maia's face. Her sister really did know her well. "That's what it's all about with TJ, isn't it? Not a love match at all, but an escape from Afi's matchmaking. You have no intention of marrying him."

In spite of herself, she flushed. It had started out that way, but lately she'd been thinking about TJ more and more. Her skin heated recalling his kisses, his knowing touch. "I don't know any more what's going to happen. Except I'm not sitting around waiting to find out."

"And the food you're taking? What's that in aid of?"

"There are hungry people in this town. People who have nothing compared to how much we have."

"Let me guess. Also TJ's doing?"

She glanced down at her hands knotted in her lap. "It started out that way. Now it's something I'm doing on my own."

"I hope you know what you're about." As Maia pushed her chair back, they both heard a faint thump from somewhere inside the walls. They stared, wide-eyed at each other.

"Is that—?"

"Did you—?"

Together they rushed from the kitchen to the back staircase near the hidden entrance to the tunnel.

"I thought Afi was having the tunnels sealed," Maia said.

"I thought so too." She ran her hands along the panel where the mechanism was located. Nothing happened when she pushed the join that was supposed to move the panel.

"Let me try." Maia stepped forward but her efforts proved equally futile.

When the hotel's front door slammed they both jumped, then raced through the lobby in time to see Selene and Beckett enter the hotel.

"Did you pass anyone going out?" Maia asked. Selene and Beckett exchanged a puzzled look.

"Out of the hotel? No," Beckett said.

"What's going on?" Selene asked.

Chandra's eye caught Maia's.

"We're not quite sure. We were in the kitchen," Maia said.

Chandra interjected. "We heard a strange sound coming from behind the wall. We went to check the tunnels, but couldn't access them from inside the hotel."

Maia took up the story. "Then we heard the front door slam. But there's no one around."

"It sounds like you've taken up reading Lila's sleuth novels," Selene said mildly. "And didn't Afi promise to render the tunnels inaccessible after what happened? Preston using them to accost me, then Beckett?"

"We've all seen Afi say one thing and do another," Chandra said darkly.

"What's the matter?" Selene said teasingly. "No longer have Afi wrapped around your little finger?"

She huffed out a breath. "Just because he didn't try to pull the emporium out from underneath you."

Selene laughed. "It certainly looked that way when he first got Beckett involved. Which you'd be aware of if you weren't lost in your own little world, sneaking off at night to meet a man we can all see is bad news."

"TJ is *not* bad news." Hearing that her sisters, normally her staunchest supporters felt that way, stung. She spun toward Beckett, who was being uncharacteristically quiet. "Don't tell me you think so too?"

"I don't know the bloke well enough to have an opinion one way or another."

"Unlike my presumptuous family. Always thinking they know best." Chandra turned on her heel and started up the stairs. Let the others worry about strange noises and goings on around the hotel. She had more important things to pursue.

CHAPTER 10

As summer faded, autumn was making its way to the mountains. Dashes of red and gold as leaves changed color stood out from the vast sea of evergreens hugging the mountains. In town, the theater was nearly finished, including a back classroom where TJ could offer magic lessons to anyone with the means. The boom from immigration had had a profound effect on American theater and the general populace were hungry for entertainment. Melodramas, comedies, Burlesques, and Wild West shows all had a ready audience, and Crawford's determination to put Silver Springs Junction on the map made it the perfect spot for a permanent theater. Performers no longer need limit themselves to New York, Philadelphia and Boston to ply their trade.

TJ knew Chandra was champing at the bit to make her stage debut, but before that happened she needed time with theater folks, helping with props and costumes or training as an understudy. If he let her mount a one-woman production, with no experience, she was sure to fail. Last thing he wanted was to see her ambitions snuffed out by falling on her face. To that end, he had contacted several traveling theater groups to ask about their availability, and if there might be a for role an enthusiastic ingenue.

"Well, isn't this simply the be-all, end-all?" An unfamiliar female voice behind him echoed through the theater.

He blew out a breath. Another bored local dropping by to see what was going on in the warehouse. Unfortunate timing, as the crew was down at the river unloading a barge of furniture Callan had helped him source. Slowly he turned. It wasn't in his best interests to alienate the townsfolk, but he didn't have time to stop and satisfy their curiosity, either.

As the woman moved from the shadows, he saw she was older, doing her best to camouflage the fact. The type his father would call 'well-preserved'.

"Sorry. I'm in the middle of a few things, ma'am," he said politely, hoping she would take the hint.

"Oh, don't mind me," she said with a forced laugh. "I'll find my own way around."

"I'm afraid it's not safe to have you wander about."

When her look hardened, his eyes narrowed. Her again. The woman he'd caught sight of leaving the hotel recently pulled at his memory. Where had he seen her before that?

"I'm a close friend of the owner," she said stiffly. "I feel confident Crawford wouldn't object to me having a quick peek."

"But I would." Their eyes locked across the room.

"Good day, Adria."

TJ breathed a sigh of relief at Chandra's timely arrival. Let her be the one to send the woman on her way.

"I'm afraid TJ is correct. It's not safe being in the building. Not until the work is complete."

"Your grandfather—"

"Perhaps you hadn't heard?" Chandra's voice took on a hard edge, indicating she held little affection for the older woman. "My grandfather has no involvement with this project."

The woman cocked her head, the pose reminding him of a hungry sparrow. "That surprises me. I didn't think anything happened in town without Crawford having some say."

"Yes, well it was a surprise to us as well. Luckily a different backer saw the potential and partnered with Mr. Dirks and myself."

Adria's eyes widened. "If only I'd known. I might have become involved."

He exchanged a look with Chandra as their unwanted guest continued on what was obviously a favorite topic. "I'm all for women having the same opportunities in business as men. As long as they don't lose sight of the fact that they *are* women."

Chandra forced a smile. "I guarantee you won't see me swinging a hammer alongside the men. But when it's time to wield a paintbrush, I hope to coax my sisters to lend a hand. Especially Minerva."

Adria shot Chandra a look of disdain, which she quickly smoothed over with a tight smile. "There's a sight I'd pay good money to see."

With a brief nod to them both, she left.

Chandra turned to him. "Sorry about that. Adria tends to overstep, and Afi is too soft to put her in her place. I doubt he has the faintest idea she's still sweet on him. I wish he'd stop giving her false hope by having her round out dinner numbers and the such."

"The woman doesn't seem capable of being sweet on

anyone other than herself. Your grandfather was smart not to get embroiled with her."

"Yes, well that's a story for another day." She looked around. "I heard the furniture had arrived."

He didn't even bother to ask how she knew. Like Crawford, she had her ways. "The men are unloading it now. Are you planning to stick around and make sure they situate it properly?"

Her eyes twinkled. "As long as I'm not in the way like dear Adria."

"You could never be in the way." His words surprised him as much as the sentiment. Somewhere along the line he'd started enjoying her company. Appreciated both her keen mind and her sharp wit. He pushed away the memory of how she'd felt in his arms. Like she belonged there, filling an emptiness that had plagued him his whole life.

Flo popped her head into Crawford's study. "Sheriff Dodds is here to see you."

"Dodds. I didn't send for him. What's he want?"

"I'm sure I wouldn't know, sir."

Crawford sighed. Highly unlikely Dodds made the trip from White Sulphur Springs for the fun of it. Mayor Haynes had been on him for a while now to elect their own lawman, but he remained reluctant.

Silver Springs Junction was his town. Having a mayor was one thing. Made them look established. But once they had a lawman running things, his influence would be eroded. Up to this point, he liked to think he could handle anything untoward that came up, see that folks settled things quietly among themselves. Which is why the sheriff knew nothing about the hotel robberies. Last thing he wanted was a bunch of clown deputies nosing around, spooking hotel guests.

He stood as the lawman shuffled into the room, his beady eyes taking inventory. He'd never felt that the law and business enterprises went together, and Dodds reinforced that belief. Putting on his biggest smile he rounded his desk and met Dodds face to face, clasping the lawman's hand in his.

"Dodds, you old son of a gun. What brings you to our simple town?"

Dodds sniffed. "Don't see a single simple thing when it comes to the town or the hotel, Crawford."

He shrugged modestly, as if he'd been paid a tremendous compliment and waited for Dodds to get to the point of his visit.

"I've got a couple of good deputies looking to move up, if you're of a mind to see a local lawman on site. Save me this going back and forth."

"Dodds, we've had this conversation before. Silver Springs Junction is a peaceful place. We've got no need of any sort of fulltime lawman around here. Even during the festival, given all the newcomers that spent time here, everyone was law-abiding. Just here for a good time."

"Aren't you forgetting about Mathers and his wife? The couple kidnapped Beckett Thompson and tried to kill you."

"We handled things just fine," he said. "Thanks again for dragging those two layabouts out of here quietly."

"You're lucky you've got Bolton. The man is quick on his feet."

He nodded, waiting.

"Shame he wasn't quick enough to stop a recent break-in here in town."

"Break-in?" Surely Dodds didn't know about the thieves who'd broken into hotel rooms innumerable times since they opened. It hadn't happened in a while and he was confident, whoever they were, they'd been just passing through and were now long gone.

"The widow Markle came to see me. Seems she was off on one of her jaunts. Came back to find her home had been broken into. Thieves made off with valuable baubles and art work."

He sat down heavily. "She didn't tell me."

"Don't know why she would. It's not like you're in a position to do anything about it. Even if you did find out who was responsible. And don't tell me you take care of your own. There's laws about vigilante justice."

That might be, but not everyone abided by the law.

"I appreciate you taking the time to stop by. Do you have any leads to the Markle break-in?"

"Not yet," Dodds said.

"Thieves are probably long gone."

"Either that or it's someone local, lying low for now, biding his time before moving the spoils out East to sell."

"I can personally vouch for anyone who's been here a while."

Dodds gave him a hard look. "Consider this a courtesy call, Crawford. A courtesy I'd appreciate extended my way if you hear anything that might pertain to the break-in. That emporium you built across the street is bound to bring in some shady characters."

"I'll let you know if I hear of anything I think you ought to check out." He stood and walked Dodds to the door, signaling the end of their meeting. Then he sent for Bolton.

~

CHANDRA SKIPPED DOWN THE STREET, excited to share her news with TJ. It turned out Mr. Lyon knew a retired stage actress from New York living the next town over. To her delight, the journalist had arranged for her to meet the woman the following day in White Sulphur Springs. It didn't matter whether or not TJ shared her excitement. It proved she was serious about her work on stage, something he seemed to dismiss as a whim of the moment on her part.

Normally, when she stopped in at the theater, she found him hard at work perfecting the space with a vision of his own. What was he doing reading a newspaper? He glanced up. His smile warmed her innards. Their last kiss had left her hungry for more.

"What's captured your interest?" she asked, plopping into the seat next to him. "I didn't know you were keeping up with what's happening around the country."

"Callan was just here and left me a few copies of papers his company publishes. He thought I'd be interested in this latest. He pushed the paper toward her. The headline jumped off the page.

Golden Age of touring for American Theater.

"What does it mean?" she asked idly as she skimmed the article.

Since 1880 An average of 250–300 shows, many originating in New York, crisscross the country each year.

"It means our timing could not be better. There are more acts to solicit than we could ever book in here. Melodrama. Vaudeville. Comedies. Operas. Musicals."

She straightened. "What of serious drama? This era has

fostered some amazing playwrights." She had personally been studying the work of Augustin Daly along with other notables.

He pushed a second headline at her.

Failure of the American playwright.

The story went on to blame emigration in the late nineteenth century, the social upheaval and innovation, along with communication and transportation as all having a profound effect on American theater.

"People want entertainment. Your grandfather figured that out. Hence the festival. In order to be successful, we need to follow his lead. To give people what they want. Callan thinks so too."

She flicked the paper disdainfully with one finger. "Callan controls what the papers print. He essentially tells people what to think. Tells them what they want."

He got to his feet, looking down at her with a serious expression. "I want us to be successful. If theater goers are willing to pay up to thirty cents a seat to be entertained, I intend to provide that entertainment. There's one theater in Ohio that sees an audience of up to forty-five thousand people a month."

She made a scoffing noise. "I'm with Afi. If people read something often enough, they start to believe it's true. I never thought I'd see you fall victim of such manipulation."

He crossed his arms over his impressive chest. With his sleeves rolled past the elbows, she could see the ridges of work-hardened muscles in his upper arms. The sight sent her insides into somersaults. "What? You're the only one who's allowed to manipulate me?"

"I did no such thing."

"Aren't you forgetting our 'betrothal'?"

"It's not like you didn't benefit." She stood as she spoke. "Look around. You wouldn't have gotten this anywhere without me. You'd still be making the rounds with your father in that worn out caravan. Maybe even still be in jail."

His eyes hardened. "Seems I misjudged you, Chandra. Shame on me." Then he pushed past her and climbed the steps two at a time to his sleeping loft.

CHAPTER 11

C handra sat down and pulled the papers toward her. As she read story after story, a sinking feeling pulled at her nether regions. Even taking Callan's control into consideration, the stories could not be all hearsay and exaggeration. Or as Afi was fond of saying, 'Where there's smoke, there's fire'.

She drummed her fingers on the table top. No way was she abandoning her dream. But based on this, she might need to change her strategy of how to go about it. She had time.

She blew out a breath. Look at her. Thinking like a grownup. Rising, she started toward the stairs to the loft. Her remark about TJ's jailtime had been a low blow. Even for her. He'd confided in her, and she'd broken his trust.

Worse yet, her reaction stemmed from a place of fear. Fear of not being seen. Of having nothing to show for her existence except a wardrobe full of out-of-date clothing, patted on the head by everyone in her family.

Upstairs, she tiptoed down the corridor and paused. TJ's accommodations looked vastly different from last time she'd been up here. He'd created a comfortable space out of what started as nothing. He had a real bed. Some sort of built-in closet. A desk. Shelves crammed with books. Curtains at the window. A walnut bureau was topped with a washing pitcher and basin. The setting was a far cry from the caravan he'd spent his entire life in. A colorful rug covered the floor and muffled the sound of her footsteps as she entered, knocking on the half-open door as she did.

He lay on the bed, eyes wide open, staring at the ceiling, arms stacked beneath his head. At her entry, he pushed himself upright, feet planted on the floor. Wary eyes followed her as she crossed the room and stared out the window.

"It's nice in here. I didn't realize you'd fixed it up." She spoke without turning around. She couldn't bear to see his expression. Didn't want to know if it registered disgust. Disappointment. Or worst of all, nothing.

"What did you expect? That I'd be living like those men in the camp? Nothing but the clothes on my back and a ragged blanket."

"I—" She gripped the windowsill, ashamed to admit she hadn't thought about how he lived. Hadn't given him much consideration other than a means to her end.

She turned to find him behind her. How had he moved without her hearing a thing?

"How will—How do you plan to stay warm in the winter?"

He sidled closer on silent feet. She stared, mesmerized by the enticing rise and fall of his chest beneath his shirt, the movement of his Adam's apple in the strong column of his throat. Her pulse clamored. Her breath rose and fell in tandem with his.

"A warm body next to me tends to do the trick. Have you

ever shared body heat with another? You might start off trying to stay warm but eventually—" White teeth flashed in a provocative look that told her he was no stranger to the experience of which he spoke.

It also told her she needed a lot more practice in the art of seducing a man.

And no time like the present to start.

She swayed against him. Rested her palms flat against his chest. She tried not to act startled when she felt a pebbling beneath her fingertips where they brushed his male breast.

His breath snagged, hot against her feverish brow. His dark eyes bored into hers.

"You know what you're doing, I hope? Approaching a man in his bed chamber." He ploughed his hands through her hair, loosening its confines, tilting her head to line up with his as he bent toward her. "Moistening your lips. Begging for my kiss. My touch. My possession."

A thrill chased through her. "I've been longing for your kiss, ever since the last one."

"I know you have."

"Then why—?"

His smile was wolfish. His grip gentled. Became a caress as his strong fingers filtered through her hair, sparking a thousand pleasure points against her scalp. "Why should you always get things your way?"

The top two buttons of his shirt were unfastened and she gripped the inside edges of the fabric, culling pleasure from the brush of her knuckles against his warm, hair roughened skin. "Because I like to?"

"You might like to. You in no way deserve it." She held her breath as his mouth found hers, a gentle force in the way his lips coaxed hers apart. A force she reacted to eagerly. Past caring if her enthusiasm was ladylike or not. She wanted— She needed—

"I say, anyone around?" A familiar male voice echoed from down below.

She leapt from his arms as if burned. "Oh, my lord. It's Afi."

Her hands flew to her head, trying vainly to smooth her hair.

He caught her hands in his. "It's a wasted effort. Anyone who sees you will know you've been thoroughly kissed. Now you've been discovered alone in a man's bedchamber. It's a good thing your grandfather believes we are betrothed. Our actions will be less of a shock. And more convincing."

She took several deep breaths as he clattered down the steps first, hurrying to catch up as he reached the main floor. "Mr. Crawford. We weren't expecting you."

Afi's gaze traveled from TJ's partly unfastened shirt to her disheveled state. "So it would appear." She waited for his lecture to follow, surprised when it didn't.

Instead, Afi turned his attention to the theater. She squinted in an effort to see it through his eyes. Would it pass muster? Or fall short of his expectations?

She gave herself a mental shake. Wasn't working her way free of familial expectations what this exercise was all about? Confidently she strolled toward him. "I gather the improvements meet your standards?"

Afi took his time, turning in a slow circle. Chandra knew his eyes didn't miss a detail. The center stage. The lighting. The seating. The rich fabric draped across the back walls, giving the whole interior the look of Aladdin's Cave or a sorcerer's lair.

"Most interesting."

"It's important patrons suspend disbelief the second

they enter." She flashed TJ a silent apology at parroting his words, treating them like her own.

"I would say that's been achieved. I hope I'm not too late with my offer."

"What offer is that?" Chandra was grateful to TJ for remaining silent in the background. For letting her hold her own with the man who raised her.

"I've had time to rethink my hasty withdrawal of support. You and I are family. Family supports each other. Despite differing opinions."

TJ cleared his throat and stepped forward. "We appreciate the lease of the warehouse, Mr. Crawford, and I'm gratified you approve our vision. But the truth is, Chandra and I secured financial backing from a different source."

Afi's eyes narrowed. "What source would that be?"

"Someone who prefers to remain anonymous at this time."

Afi's gaze cut to her. "You wouldn't dare have gone to Callan Douglas?"

She didn't bother to deny the accusation. For all the good it would do. Afi wouldn't rest until he learned the truth. She reached for TJ's hand. "Ruthless in matters of business. Is that not one of your oft-stated creeds?"

Could that be grudging admiration in the look Afi sent her?

"I fear I have given you far too much freedom in your youth. All of you girls." He shot TJ a pointed look. "Do we need to hurry along the wedding plans?"

She chimed in before TJ could answer. "Selene would never forgive me, Afi. It's only right she marries before I do."

Afi turned, shaking his head as he did so. "I will not rest easy until I see all four of you wed." He paused and glanced over his shoulder to include them both in a dark glance.

"Remember. A betrothal is a far cry from an exchange of vows. As for you, Chandra. I have missed seeing you around the hotel. With things nearing completion here, do you think we might once more be graced with your presence? Selene was complaining that you are never around to help with the plans for her big day."

"I promise, I will be more present."

"I'll see to it," TJ added.

Afi's expression was unreadable as he plopped his hat onto his head. "You and your sisters will be the death of me. As for the two of you, be careful in your dealings with Douglas."

CHANDRA WIPED damp palms on her skirt before lifting her hand to the elaborate brass door knocker shaped like a serpent. Ever since getting off the train she could smell sulphur, the mineral in the springs that gave the town of White Sulphur Springs its name. Even though she was expected she couldn't still her nerves, all but holding her breath as the door swung open.

"Miss Crawford?" The older woman's voice was clear and melodious, her smile gracious and obviously well-practiced. Chandra could imagine the actress's voice projected through one of the many theater houses in Philadelphia or New York.

"Miss Danford." She felt like she ought to curtsey in the presence of such talent. "I was delighted when Mr. Lyon told me you were willing to meet with me."

"Victoria, please. I admit, to being curious when I heard from Mr. Lyon. I didn't know he'd kept tabs on me since I moved West."

"Mr. Lyon is full of surprises." Chandra took a breath, unsure where to start her well-rehearsed speech. "I don't know how much he told you, but I've recently become involved in starting a theater in Silver Springs Junction. I plan to take to the stage there myself."

Her companion nodded. "I heard about the theater. Lots of talk in these parts about Silver Springs Junction, the Emporium and the festival. Please tell me you're not here to try and lure me out of retirement. My husband would kill me."

"Nothing like that," she said as she was shown into a tastefully appointed parlor. The mantle above the fireplace held a half a dozen framed likenesses of the actress during her career, and she resisted the urge to cross the room to study them up close. Instead, she took the seat her hostess indicated. "Do you ever miss the stage?"

Just then a maid appeared with a tea tray which she set onto a side table. "Thank you, Jess," Victoria said. Turning back to Chandra she waved a hand to encompass her surroundings. "Do I miss it? Certain aspects, to be sure. Not enough to give up all this."

She drew a breath. "I don't really know where to start. I've been drawn to the stage ever since I was a young girl. We moved a lot and I was always thrilled when the new town had some sort of theater. Our governess was a keen theatergoer." Oh, lord she was babbling.

Victoria merely appeared amused.

Changing tactics, Chandra fumbled in her bag. "I've written a few stage plays." Over twenty, but who was counting. "Fairly simple productions. I was hoping you'd have time to look over one or two and give me some feedback."

Victoria reached for the folded pages. "I'm no playwright. As I'm sure you're aware, the entertainment industry changed markedly before I left. Theatergoers are now happier with vaudeville over Shakespeare. Slapstick over serious."

"I know," Chandra said. "I'd like to bring back some of the traditional styles of storytelling and acting, but in a more modern fashion that will appeal to today's audience. I could really use your help."

Victoria smiled broadly. "Let's have our tea, shall we? Then you can tell me exactly what you have in mind."

AS THE THEATER NEARED COMPLETION, TJ had time to turn his attention to the magic school, which he was calling The Magic Stage. He'd set up a small classroom on one side of the warehouse, originally intended for use as the warehouse office. He'd furnished it simply with a row of chairs and a couple of large wooden tables. Two trunks filled with props his father had left behind were stacked against the far wall.

Since the festival, Silver Springs Junction had grown by leaps and bounds. It seemed every train that arrived in town brought a new influx of settlers, just the way old Crawford had envisioned. Capitalizing on that fact, TJ anticipated a future where keen students of all ages were eager to learn how to entertain their family and friends with a repertoire of simple magic tricks. Last week a note had been slipped under the Magic Stage's door, requesting a lesson from a few of the newcomers, stating a specific day and time.

He arrived early and began to get ready, setting the front table with a few simple props. A couple of decks of cards. Gold bands. A top hat. A magic box from which items appeared and disappeared. The door opened quietly behind him. As he turned to greet his students, he saw the heavy wooden club heading his way seconds before it connected with his skull.

"NICE TO HAVE YOU BACK," Selene said, with a pointed look toward Chandra. The four sisters were gathered on the same discarded settees in what had recently become a full-blown artist's studio. She was happy to see Minerva taking herself and her art more seriously these days, the same way she was approaching her acting. Which included spending a lot of time with Victoria Danford.

"Miss me?" She flashed Selene a cheeky smile. She could afford to feel generous these days, now that she had a renewed sense of purpose.

Selene gave a disapproving cluck with her tongue and slid a swatch of fabric toward her. "We chose this for the attendants' dresses." She arched a brow. "Shame you weren't here to help decide. Just don't expect me to bend over backwards to help when it's your turn."

"Sorry." Her sisters still thought she intended to marry TJ. She needed to take a cue from Selene, learn how an excited bride-to-be acted. She fingered the fabric, a claret-colored brocade that should flatter all of them. "I approve your choice."

"How kind," Selene said sarcastically.

"Girls." Maia stepped into her older-sister role. "We're here to help ensure Selene's special day is everything she hopes for. And Chandra is committed to do her part. Isn't that right?" She leveled a pointed look toward Chandra.

"Whatever I can do to help," she said.

"How about you stop disappearing? The dressmaker is due to arrive any day to take measurements and do fittings."

Her heart plummeted. So much for escaping to White Sulphur Springs to spend time with Victoria Danford. As her sisters' voices ran together in an animated discussion of flowers, decorations, refreshments and the bridal waltz, she wondered how soon before she could leave. She was anxious to check in with TJ and see how he was coming along booking performers. They hoped to open next month and there was still so much to do. After what felt like forever, the wedding planning session wrapped up. She lost no time excusing herself.

"You really can't stay away from that man of yours, can you?" Minerva said.

"Selene," she implored her sister. "Help me out. These two don't know what's like to be in love."

Selene gave her a pointed look. "I'm not sure you do either."

She raised her chin. "You didn't even like Beckett when you two first met."

"Let's just say he grew on me over time. I don't necessarily believe in love at first sight, the way you claim happened between you and TJ."

To her surprise, Maia came to her defense. "Chandra will follow her heart, wherever it leads."

She shot Maia a grateful look, even as she felt a twinge of guilt at misleading her sisters. As youngsters, the four of them had always been so close. As the years passed, the others seemed content with their lot, unlike her. Longing to escape a town where everyone knew she was a Crawford.

As she scampered down the hill toward town, she mentally reviewed the list of things she needed to discuss with TJ. Having handbills printed was a priority. Luckily a printer had moved to town last month and set up shop. Along with new buildings popping up everywhere.

She stopped momentarily to watch a group of construction workers, wondering if they had been hired by Afi or worked for Callan. Either way, Afi was seeing his dream of turning a railway junction into a bustling town come true right before his eyes. Same as her with her acting.

Just inside the theater she froze. The backwall curtains had been ripped from their hangings. Tables and chairs had been overturned or smashed. Leftover paint had been flung about, defacing the interior. Huge gaping holes could be seen in the stage floor, as if someone had chopped through with an axe.

TJ! She flew up the steps to his sleeping loft. The room was empty and untouched. Fear choked her throat, making it impossible to call out. She remembered Beckett being snatched up and nearly killed by a pair of lunatics intent on revenge.

Racing back downstairs, she heard a faint shuffle from the far side of the stage "Who's there?" she called authoritatively in her best stage voice, one she'd been practicing with Victoria. "Show yourself this second."

A man crawled slowly from beneath one of the tables. His clothing was ragged, his hands and face filthy. She was too angry to feel afraid.

"Did you do this?" she demanded as he stood.

He shook his head vehemently.

"I know you," she said, studying him as she advanced slowly. "You saved that newborn kitten." As if on cue, Shakespeare appeared and wrapped her tail around the man's ankles, as if backing up his innocence.

He stared down at his feet.

"Were you in here? Did you see who did this?"

He looked at her, wide-eyed. "I don't want no trouble."

"You're not in trouble. I know you're a good person. But

you must have seen what happened. Did something happen to TJ? Did the bad people take him?"

He shook his head.

"Can you take me to him?"

Shakespeare sat and started grooming herself as the man turned and limped toward the door. Chandra hurried to keep up as they circled the building to the entrance of the Magic Stage. "In there."

She pushed open the door to see TJ lying near the far wall in a pool of blood. She gasped and rushed to kneel at his side, relieved to see the rise of fall of his chest. He was still alive.

She turned to the door. "Don't just stand there. Go get help." But the hobo was nowhere in sight.

CHAPTER 12

TJ groaned. Thank God he was gaining consciousness. Reaching under her skirt, she tore a strip off her petticoat. She pressed the fabric against a ragged gash that started in the center of his forehead and ended near his temple. She swallowed thickly as the white fabric turned pink beneath her fingers. TJ winced. His eyes fluttered open. He blinked, focused on her, then immediately tried to sit. She placed a firm hand on his shoulder, holding him there.

"Lie still. You've been attacked."

He sucked in his breath, exhaled, and closed his eyes.

"Who?" he asked, barely moving his lips.

"I don't know. I just found you. Actually, one of the hobos was in the theater. He brought me here."

"Buckshot," TJ said.

"Buckshot? No, you were hit with something. Something big and heavy, judging by the wound on your forehead. It's the size of a goose's egg." She was relieved to see the injury had just about stopped bleeding. Already his swollen forehead was turning a nasty violet color.

TJ opened his eyes. Despite her protests, he struggled to

a seated position propped against the wall. He breathed heavily, indicating the effort that small move required. She'd never manage to get him to the doctor on her own.

"We need to get you seen to," she said briskly as she sat back on her heels. "Will you be all right alone if I go fetch the doctor? I won't be long. Promise you won't try to get up."

"No promises," he said heavily.

"TJ." She bit her lower lip. Better she told him sooner than later. "Whoever it was, they messed up the theater pretty good."

"Did Buckshot see who it was? He was in there."

"Buckshot?"

"Older man from the hobo camp. Walks with a limp. They call him Buckshot because he has a leg full of the stuff. It's hard for him to jump on and off the trains anymore so he mostly sticks around town."

"The one who rescued the kitten?"

"That's him."

"What was he doing here?"

"I feed him. Sometimes he hangs around and helps sweeping up and stuff. He's harmless."

Just then they were interrupted by the loud rap of knuckles against the doorframe. She jumped to her feet. "Dr. Hilliard. Thank goodness."

"Chandra." The doctor she'd seen many a time sipping whisky with her grandfather frowned as he entered. "I'm surprised to see you here. One of those bums from the camp showed up at my infirmary. Babbled incessantly. Wouldn't leave until I collected my bag and followed him."

"TJ was attacked," she said. "He was unconscious when I got here."

The doctor switched his attention to TJ. "It's probably not as bad as it looks. Head wounds tend to bleed a lot.

Young man, if Chandra and I both give you a hand, do you think we can get you up on the table so I can have a good look at you?"

"I would have gotten up already if Chandra would let me."

"Best not to rush these things." The doctor set his bag down on a nearby chair. "I'll take one side of him, Chandra. You grab hold under his other arm. Slowly. Easy does it. We don't want him going back down."

She reached down and hooked one arm beneath TJ's underarm. He winced, used the wall behind him for support and slowly straightened. She managed to slip her shoulder where her hand had been and take some of his weight by slinging his arm across her shoulders.

The doctor did the same on the other side, his face red from the exertion. "Don't try to walk yet," he told TJ. "Just get used to the feel of your legs underneath you to start. Okay? Say when you're ready."

"Ready," TJ said through gritted teeth. Slowly they shuffled him to the table. He grabbed hold and clung to the side, knuckles white. "Can I just sit in a chair?"

"I'd prefer you lying on the table. I'm pretty sure that gash on your head will need a stitch or two. Don't touch," he cautioned when TJ tried to raise a hand to the injury. "We need to keep things as sterile as possible." He looked at Chandra. "Any chance of some hot water so I can clean him up and see what we're dealing with?"

She looked at TJ.

"Should be some in the pot over the fire out back."

"That'll do," the doctor said. "Now let's get you onto the table."

She paused in the doorway to look back. Already, TJ had lost that deathly white look as his face regained some of its color. He seemed steadier as he sank onto the table and swung his legs up after him. She left as the doctor was easing him to a prone position.

At the fire, a blackened pot sat over a few glowing coals. As a faint stream of steam rose from inside it and dissipated into the air, she felt a flush of shame. She knew so little of how he lived while the warehouse was being transformed. The wooden handle was cool to her touch, so she picked up the entire pot and hurried back, careful not to spill its contents.

Doc Hilliard didn't look up at her return, just waved a hand toward an empty chair. "Set it there."

As she followed his request, she caught sight of TJ's chest and gasped. Water sloshed over the edge of the pot as she set it down with an unsteady hand, unable to look away.

TJ's shirt was unbuttoned, displaying a mottled purple and red marbling across his torso. He gritted his teeth as the doctor pressed his middle with both hands, none-too-gently from what she could tell.

"You're hurting him."

"Chandra." TJ's voice was low, warning her to mind her own business. "Let the doc do his job."

"Feels like you have a cracked rib or two," the doctor said, straightening. He pulled a hunk of white cloth from his bag, dipped it in the hot water and began to wipe the smeared blood from TJ's face and hair. "You say you never saw what hit you?"

"Only caught a glimpse from the corner of my eye. It looked like some sort of club or bat."

"From the look of you, whoever it was had it out for you. They weren't content with knocking you out, but must have taken several swings after you went down." The doc looked at Chandra. "Maybe you can help convince your grandfather that this town would benefit from a fulltime lawman. Takes too long to send to White Sulphur Springs. And as long as we've got those hobos hanging around—"

"This wasn't hobos," TJ said.

"So you say. Chandra get over here and give the man your hand to squeeze. This is going to smart some when I sew him up."

"Is that really necessary?" TJ said.

"Sewing you up? Or hanging on to Chandra while I do it?"

"I was referring to the sewing aspect. I'd rather let it heal on its own."

"You think women prefer the rugged, battered look? Take it from me. They'll like you a whole lot better after I stitch you up. Sporting a bandage ought to get you a fair amount of sympathy. Isn't that right, Chandra? Most women can't resist a man who needs a spot of nursing."

As he spoke, the doctor dabbed at the gash on TJ's head, which didn't look nearly as bad as when she first saw him. She slipped her fingers into TJ's hand and looked away as the doctor went about the business of putting him back together. He gave her fingers a gentle squeeze, not the bone-crushing grip she was expecting, but a surprisingly gentle pressure. As if *he* was reassuring *her*.

"All done." The doctor unwrapped a surgical dressing and stuck it over his handiwork. "Great inventions these adhesive plasters. Told your grandfather I wish I'd come up with the knowhow. I'd be a millionaire like him." He laughed as he packed his bag and snapped it shut. He helped TJ sit up, then clapped him on one shoulder. "Come see me in a week or so. I'll take out the stitches and we'll see what kind of dashing scar you have to regale the ladies with stories of your bravery."

TJ sent Chandra an amused look. "Thank you, doctor." He pulled a handful of bills from his pocket. "How much do I owe you?"

"We'll settle up when you come to the infirmary next week. Chandra, give my best to Crawford. Unless you don't want him to know you're spending time with the likes of this fellow." He poked TJ on the shoulder as if he was making a joke.

Chandra stiffened. "Afi knows I'm here."

The doctor gave her an indulgent smile. "Yes, he tells me you two have big plans."

"He told you that?"

"Crusty as he pretends to be, deep down he's proud of you. Not that he'd say as much to your face, mind, but he's always bragging about 'his girls'. Maia running the hotel as good as any man. Selene and her emporium endeavor, with wedding plans in the offing. Minerva's dedication to her art. He was worried about you for a while there, but told me he's secretly happy you've found your niche." He paused at the door. "Besides, I think it was a blight on his record, this building sitting empty this past year. Showed folks he wasn't always right with his predictions for the future. Then you came along and saved face. Next thing he'll be claiming he intended for it to be a theater all along. Was just waiting for you to be ready."

And didn't that just sound like Afi! "Thank you, doctor, for everything."

The second the door closed behind the man, she turned to TJ. "I think you ought to stay at the hotel for the time being."

"I'm not staying at the hotel." TJ hefted himself to his feet, then held the table to steady himself.

"But whoever did this might come back."

"Next time I'll be ready for them." He let go of the table and started unsteadily toward the door.

"Where are you going? The doctor said you need to rest."

"I need to see what kind of damage they did next door. And hunt down Buckshot. Find out if he saw who it was."

"You can't go traipsing around out there. You've got one or more cracked ribs plus a head wound. Please come up to the hotel. At least for the rest of the day. I'll have Cook fix you some healing soup," she added in her most persuasive voice.

"Some things can't be fixed by a warm bed and a bowl of soup."

Stubborn man! She followed him from the classroom to the theater, where he stooped to right a knocked over chair. She heard him suck in his breath at the movement. It must have hurt. Maybe now he'd listen to her.

His face tightened as he slowly turned in a circle, surveying the space. She gnawed her lip. "Could have been worse," was all he said.

"You've seen it. Now will you please come back to the hotel with me? We can figure out what we need to do to repair the damage. Order more wall fabric and fresh paint."

Two long strides brought him to her side. You'd never know he was injured. He cupped her face in his hands and tilted it toward his. The white plaster was pale against his skin, and gave him a rough and tumble look. Maybe Doctor Hilliard had been right. Maybe women were drawn to men in need of their care. She smoothed his forearm beneath the fabric of his shirt, remembering how vulnerable he looked lying on the table, bruised and bleeding.

"Let me take care of you," she said.

TJ barked out a laugh, which had to have hurt. "Somehow, I don't see nursing as one of your talents, Chandra. But I appreciate the offer." He leaned down and brushed his lips against hers. Automatically she reached for him, tried to wrap her arms around his middle, keep him close. He sucked in his breath and released her.

"I expect I'll be sore for a few days, yet."

Her arms fell to her sides. "Of course. I'm sorry."

"Don't act all meek, either. It doesn't suit you."

"Oh!" She huffed out an exasperated breath. "I'm trying to help you."

"No, you're not. You're trying to get your own way. Same as always. Now why don't you run along and talk to the printer about those handbills you've been on about? Let me go see what I can find out from Buckshot. He may have gone into hiding."

"How will you find him if he has?"

"Leave that to me."

Men! Why did they always insist everything be left to them?

TJ PICKED his way carefully down the sloping bank to the hobo camp. Not for the world would he admit every move hurt like the blazes, even leaning in to kiss the worried frown from Chandra's lips. There was no part of his body that didn't ache. He flexed his fingers. Sore but not broken. A small thing to be grateful for. Without the manual dexterity he'd perfected over the years, there would be no magic trick he'd be able to perform, let alone teach others.

At the camp, a small group huddled around a smoky fire. Inquiring after Buckshot got him either a puzzled frown or a weak shrug of the shoulders. Hardly surprising. The men here kept to themselves and trusted no one. Not even each other. A feeling he remembered well.

He eventually found Buckshot on the far reaches of the camp, sheltered beneath a lean-to made from a few rough branches and a bundle of rags, so well-camouflaged he nearly walked right past it. Buckshot lay huddled in a ball, as if by taking up as little room as possible no one would see him.

He was too sore to lean over, so settled for giving Buckshot's foot a gentle nudge with his. Buckshot stirred and angled his head toward him, the whites of his eyes the one thing that made him appear human. Yet, he knew that beneath that sallow chest beat a pure heart.

He touched the plaster on his forehead. "You saw the men who tried to kill me? The ones who trashed the theater?"

Buckshot shifted till he was sitting up, arms wrapped around bony knees that formed a ledge he rested his chin upon, watching him warily. After some hesitation, he nodded. "Bad men."

"They were bad men. Have you seen them around any other time? Could you point them out?"

He shook his head.

"Not from here, then?" TJ couldn't keep the discouraged tone from his voice.

Buckshot's voice was gravelly from lack of use. "Gone."

"Gone? You mean left town? You saw them get on the train?"

Buckshot nodded.

Which meant they could have gone anywhere. Never to be seen again.

Buckshot made a few incoherent noises which he had learned meant he was struggling for the right words.

"Take your time," he said encouragingly. "The words will come."

Buckshot tried a few syllables. Then he tugged on his shabby, torn jacket. "Fancy."

"They were fancy-dressed," TJ said. "Like foreigners?"

Buckshot pressed his lips together. Made a few hand-gestures that looked like he was drawing castles in the sky.

The message was lost on him. Then it struck.

"City folk. Men from out East. Not from around here?"

Buckshot's eyes lit up as he nodded eagerly.

"Thanks, buddy." Even though it hurt, he gave Buckshot a grateful pat on the head. Now he needed to figure out why a couple of well-dressed thugs from the city would be hanging around Silver Springs Junction, let alone bother to rough him up, along with the theater.

AFTER LEAVING TJ, Chandra stopped at the printers. Thanks to her friend Victoria, she had a sample of a fancy handbill from a theater out East. It would at least give the printer some idea of how she wanted the handbills to look. From there she hesitated, tempted to go check on TJ. Instead, she turned toward the hotel. He was right. Fussing didn't suit her. She hadn't gone far before the family carriage passed her and stopped. The door opened and Minerva poked her head out. "Fancy a lift?"

So much for rehearsing her latest character study.

She plopped down across from Minerva and Selene, next to a stranger, a woman of indeterminate age with hair an unnaturally bright shade of red.

"Lillian has graciously agreed to come here to make our dresses, instead of us having to go to her," Selene said.

Lillian chortled, her fleshy chin bobbing. "Happy to do it. I've heard so much about Silver Springs Junction and the new Emporium; nice to see it with my own eyes. Who knows? I might even give my luck a try while I'm here."

Chandra leaned toward the dressmaker. "I was wondering—Would it be possible to measure me first?"

Lillian turned to Selene. "That would be up to the bride."

"Honestly, Chandra," Selene said. "I am sick and tired of your selfish ways. As youngest, you will be the last one to have your dress made. And I expect your full support and attention while Lillian fits the rest of us."

Too late to escape back to the theater.

Maia greeted them at the hotel's entrance, where Selene introduced Lillian. "Let me show you to your room. It's a nice quiet one on the back of the hotel."

"Yes, not like all the construction noise down near the station," Chandra said to no one in particular.

Maia stiffened. "That dreadful Mr. Douglas has some nerve. Now he's building his own hotel."

News to her. "What does Afi think about that?"

"You know Afi. Always with his own agenda. He claims there's enough business for everyone. That prosperity begets more prosperity."

That sounded like Afi.

Unlikely she'd echo those same sentiments should Callan Douglas suddenly decide the town could support two theaters.

CHAPTER 13

As each day passed, moving hurt less. The doctor removed his stitches, and although one eyebrow appeared a little off-kilter, his bruises faded. Chandra hadn't been around much, which was fine with him. He welcomed the days and nights of hard work, slowly erasing all traces of destruction in the theater.

To his surprise, Crawford made arrangements for him to visit the school one afternoon and dazzle the children with a few simple tricks. The delight and enthusiasm of the students was contagious. Would Crawford have paid him such an honor if the old man knew his betrothal to Chandra was a hoax?

"Hope I'm not interrupting?"

TJ stiffened and turned slowly, still trying not to jump every time someone entered the theater. As the newcomer moved into the light he recognized Beckett, the man betrothed to one of Chandra's sisters. He was still having difficulty sorting the women out, even though they appeared different in looks and temperament. According to Chandra, Beckett had come to town to help set up the gambling hall, then been abducted and trapped inside a burning building. Saved only by his quick thinking and the fast actions of his lady love.

He wiped his oily hands on a cleaning rag before extending a hand to his visitor. "Beckett, right? Soon to marry into the Crawford clan?"

"I've been meaning to stop by sooner," Beckett said, "but something always seems to crop up."

"I know the feeling."

Facing the other man, he was acutely aware of his humble beginnings, his nomadic life, his incarceration. Beckett was dressed in a suit of clothing befitting a man soon to marry a granddaughter of the town's founding family. While TJ was, and always would be a nobody. Except when he was on stage. But that performer, who easily held an audience spellbound, wasn't the real him. "What can I do for you?" He doubted Beckett was here for a private magic lesson.

"This is somewhat awkward, given we don't know each other. But it is the request of my soon-to-be wife that I enlist you as one of my groomsmen. You'll be matched with her sister Chandra to even out the numbers."

"Your betrothed wants me to be one of the wedding party?"

Beckett made a self-deprecating face. "Women are better at things like this. I thought all I needed was a best man to hand me the ring. Goes to show what I know. Apparently even numbers are in order, one groomsman to pair with every attendant, and as she has three sisters—"

He laughed and stuck out his hand. One never knew when it would be useful to have a friend in town. "I would be honored."

Beckett clasped his hand with genuine warmth. "Happy to return the favor when it's your turn to take the plunge."

"I'll remember that." No point telling Beckett such a day wasn't in the cards.

Beckett shoved his hands in his pockets and took a long, assessing look around. "It's quite the transformation you've made here."

"Thank you." He surprised himself by adding, "Would you like me to show you around?"

As the two men toured the building, conversation between them never faltered, and before he left Beckett extracted a promise from TJ to join him and the other groomsmen that evening. Apparently, a fancy tailor was in town to see to their wedding costumes.

"The girls have been tied up for weeks with some dress-maker from out East. Seems now it's our turn. See you tonight."

So that's why he hadn't seen hide nor hair of Chandra. Not that he'd been missing her flighty ways. The woman couldn't hold a thought in her head longer than a minute, and was constantly leaping from one thing to the next in a way that made his head hurt. He'd been evasive when she quizzed him about the acts he'd booked so far because he knew she wouldn't approve his choices. Luckily her attention had quickly moved on.

He'd been conservative with the acts who'd appear until they got established. Given her way, Chandra would see a different performer every night of the week, but the town was in its infancy. People were barely settled. Few had the necessary coins to fill the theater every night.

The festival had been wildly successful because most of the entertainment had been free, with Old man Crawford investing a king's ransom to ensure the event's success. The theater would be a slow build for performers as well as theatergoers.

"TJ. Is it true?"

He blew out a breath. How was it possible that thinking about Chandra brought her to his side?

"Is what true?"

"That Beckett asked you to be a groomsman."

Apparently there were no secrets in the Crawford family. Well, only one. That his betrothal to Chandra was a wild concoction from that impulsive mind of hers.

"And you said yes?"

He couldn't help but smile. She was as excited as a little girl, all but jumping up and down, her eyes shining.

"I take it you approve? I wasn't altogether sure you would, but I couldn't see a gracious way to decline."

"Silly. Of course I approve. The wedding will be far more fun with you there."

He wasn't so sure about that. "When is the happy day? I forgot to ask."

"Not for a couple of weeks." She made a face. "I had no idea so much work went into planning a wedding. Far more than what we went through to get the theater ready."

She spoke as if she'd been the one slaving here day and night to bring their project to readiness. No doubt, as soon as things started to feel repetitive, she'd be gone. Flitting off to something new and shiny. Hopefully by then he'd have proven himself to Crawford and could stick around, not keep moving the way his old man had. He idly wondered if Da ever caught up to Ma, if his parents had given each other another chance.

"I almost forgot!" She reached into her bag and pulled out a sheaf of paper which she waved in his face. "I have the handbills ready to post."

"It's too soon."

"It's never too soon to get folks excited about what's in the offing. Give them time to save their pennies."

"Chandra, we agreed on October first to open our doors. That way we'll get a good first month under our belts before the weather worsens."

"Folks out East don't let a little snow deter them from seeking out their entertainment."

"There are a lot more folks living in those cities. And while people are moving West and settling here, it's happening slowly. We need to do the same. Keep pace with the town."

She batted his arm. "You are such a spoilsport. Why do you have to rain all over my ideas?"

Because they're as flighty and impulsive as she was?

He looked at her, shaking his head. He couldn't say that aloud. Any more than he could tell her she was the most frustrating, fascinating woman he had ever met. And if she kept looking at him like that, he'd have to kiss her.

In fact—

CHANDRA WASN'T sure which one of them moved first. Or did they come together in an instinct as old as time itself? An instinct where one party recognizes their 'other'. However it happened, suddenly the only thing that mattered was being in TJ's arms. His lips hungry and seeking on hers. Ferreting out her secret desires. Igniting her wants; fueling them with his.

Heavy breaths warred with moans and pants as her body found and matched the rhythm of his. His heartbeat. His kisses. His hands setting her aflame. She couldn't get enough of him. Close enough to him. She thrilled to his touch, whimpering slightly as his lips left hers, then moaning in pleasure as he laved her throat, his teeth grazing the delicate spot where neck met shoulder.

She was ready to erupt; letting out a primal sob of need and surrender. A sound he swallowed and soothed as his kiss gentled, his hold softened. She sighed in frustration. Sensing his withdrawal before it happened.

When he moved to put space between them, she caught his hand in hers. She searched his face. "What—Why—?"

He shook his head, exhaled shakily and ran his free hand through his hair. "Why did I stop? Apparently I have a few shreds of honor left in me. Bedding you would be a mistake. For both of us."

She didn't want to stop. She wanted to feel. To fully experience whatever it was she'd gotten only a tiny taste of. "Why a mistake?"

How could something that felt so right, so inevitable, ever be wrong?

"You know nothing of the world."

She stiffened, his words like a dash of cold water. He was right! How could she possibly portray emotions on stage that she had never experienced firsthand? Love. Loss. Passion. Fear. How could she expect an audience to feel those emotions along with her, if all she could project was a pale imitation?

"Show me," she said boldly. "Everything you know of the world. Of human nature."

She bit off her words, stung by the realization. Her eyes searched his. Showing her the ins and outs of life is what he'd been doing when he'd had her prepare food for the unfortunates in the hobo camp. He'd exposed her to people with far less than her, who shared what little they had.

Watched after each other. Saved the life of an abandoned kitten.

Surely there was so much more for her to see, feel, experience.

"You wouldn't want to see what I've seen, to know what I know."

"And if I disagree?"

He turned away. "The world is not a kind place, Chandra."

"Hence the need for entertainment. A respite. A distraction. An escape from reality for a short time. At the theater."

"That's exactly what we're intending."

Argh! He wasn't listening to a word she said. "How can I possibly help people escape a world I know nothing of?"

She turned and left, deflated. She was a fraud. A pampered and indulged rich girl with totally unrealistic hopes and dreams. She might as well marry the first blandly acceptable man Bolton produced. At least she'd make Afi happy.

"So that's it, then. Just like that, you're giving up."

Chandra shifted on the sofa in Victoria's parlor, wincing at the censure in her mentor's voice. "Better that than falling on my face, wouldn't you say?"

"You're in no position to make that judgement until you've fallen flat, dusted yourself off, and returned triumphant."

"Is that what happened to you?"

"Many times," Victoria said cheerfully.

"Is that why you eventually left the stage?"

Victoria gave her a pitying look. "The highs and lows are

all part of the life. Every life for that matter. On stage or off. But when I met my husband, I realized the victories had been hollow. Any perceived high points a tiny replica of what life can be like when you find true love."

She looked down at her hands, knotted in her lap. "You're saying love is different from passion?"

"Passion is fleeting. Fickle. Love is all-encompassing. It might ebb and flow with the times, but it always emerges. Better, brighter, stronger than before."

She leaned forward. "How can I possibly act a role I know nothing about? Haven't experienced firsthand?"

Victoria gave her a stern look. "Do you think the great playwrights had firsthand knowledge of everything they wrote? Any more than the actors who played the roles?"

"I guess not," she said.

Again, that all-seeing gaze reached inside her. "I sense something else is bothering you."

Something else named TJ.

"If someone else makes you feel things, is that good or is that bad?"

"It all depends. If someone makes you happy and full of joy that is good. If someone is cruel or frightens you, that is bad. You know what else is equally bad?"

She shook her head.

"Relying on others to make you feel." Victoria formed a fist and pushed it to her breastbone. "Feelings should come from here. From within. Sometimes those feelings make us uncomfortable. We ignore them or wish them away. But they are there for a reason."

"What if someone else heightens those feelings? Say, when you're happy. And just the sight of them makes you happier."

Victoria patted her hand. "Those are the best feelings."

Her smile lingered, softened. "Those are the feelings you need to bring to your work. Those are what will guarantee your audience leaves a show feeling better than when they entered. You have the power to do that."

"You think so?"

"I know so. Shall we get to work?"

TJ APPROACHED the front door of the attractive, two-story wood house, one of the first homes built between the railway station and Silver Springs Hotel, according to Chandra. A home where she had lived with her sisters and grandfather until the hotel was completed. A thin stream of smoke curled from the chimney, testimony to the cooler nights in the mountains with summer's passing into fall. He wondered how it felt. A real home. Friends who respected you. A place you belonged. A wife to share it with.

Before he could knock, the front door opened. Bolton stood there, his tie off, his vest unfastened.

"Saw you coming up the walk."

Almost as if Bolton had been waiting for him. Could he trust him? It's not like he had any other choice.

"Sorry to bother you at home. I was hoping you'd have a minute to talk."

"Come on in. My wife's up at the hotel. Wedding-fever seems to get hold of women no matter their age or circumstances. Glad such nonsense is behind me." He gave TJ a sympathetic smile. "Guess you've got that to look forward to."

For one crazy second he longed to confide in Bolton. Tell him how the whole betrothal was a hoax, concocted by Chandra for her own reasons. And how he regretted going along with it. But that wouldn't do. Best stick to the reason he was here.

"Strikes me you're the closest thing to the law in these parts."

Bolton laughed. "Never heard a retired bounty hunter credited with being on the right side of the law before." He indicated an empty chair at the square wooden table off to one side of the parlor, near the fire. It was piled with books and reams of paper, which Bolton pushed aside.

TJ shrugged. "More so than an ex-con."

"I heard you were innocent and pardoned of all wrong-doing."

"One of the lucky ones."

Bolton sat back, arms crossed over his chest. "But you're not here to rehash the past, are you?"

He shook his head. "Heard you're investigating, quietly, some jewelry thefts at the hotel."

"Chandra?" Bolton guessed.

He nodded. Then he reached into his inside pocket and pulled out a velvet bag. He spilled the contents onto the table between them. "Anything here match any descriptions of missing items?"

Bolton fingered through the gems, then looked up at him. "It's possible. Where did you get these?"

"I was going through a trunk in the Magic Stage. Looking for some props I needed. I found this tucked near the bottom."

"Ever see it before?"

He shook his head.

"Could it have been left there by your father?"

"I have a few baubles my Da left. They're in the hotel safe. No way these came from him."

"And no idea when or how they got there." He searched TJ's face. "Magic perhaps?"

"A magician is only as good as the tools he has to work with. I took an inventory of the props Da left me. In case I needed to replace anything. Nothing like this was there." He tried not to look too concerned. Problem was, he'd been framed before. Wouldn't take much to convince a judge he never should have got off; had gone back to his old ways.

Bolton crossed one booted leg across his opposite knee. "Heard you got beat up a while back by a couple of thugs. Who also damaged the theater. Any reason to think they might have been the ones to plant stolen property on you?"

"Only thing I know about them is they weren't from around here. And they lit out of town right after."

Bolton raised a brow. "You know that for sure?"

"Friend saw them trash the theater then jump on the next train out of town."

"This friend got a name?"

"Not that I'm at liberty to share."

He resisted the urge to fidget under Bolton's narrowed gaze. "What would you like me to do with this information?"

"I was hoping you could get the gemstones back to their rightful owners."

"Anyone I reach out to will want to know how they came to my hand."

"Turned in by a good Samaritan?" he said hopefully.

Bolton stared at the cache of gems scattered across the table. "I don't like this," he said finally. "It wouldn't be a stretch to think someone's gunning for you. Or trying to make you a scapegoat. Which wouldn't be hard, given your background."

"What if it's more than that?" he said, leaning forward.

Bolton raised a brow, encouraging him to go on.

"I've been thinking. If whoever beat me up wanted me dead, I wouldn't be here."

"I'm listening."

"A man like Crawford is bound to have enemies. Someone who doesn't want to see him succeed in his ventures with Silver Springs Junction. If the theater does well, it's another feather in the old man's cap." He had a mental debate with himself before adding, "Someone paid my old man to leave. Probably expected I'd go with him. But here I am."

Bolton waited for him to continue.

"Now they're either trying to scare me off, or see me arrested. If they succeed, what happens to the theater? Chandra can't continue with it on her own."

"Someone else steps in to pick up the pieces?" Bolton said.

TJ shrugged. "Possibly."

Bolton met his eyes, his thoughts hidden. Could it be they were both thinking about the same man? Someone recently moved to town. Wealthy and powerful in his own right. Possibly jealous of Crawford. And certain to have the money and power to bring in some fancy hired muscle.

Callan Douglas.

Who just happened to be a silent partner in the theater.

CHAPTER 14

"Such a shame no one from Beckett's family will be at the wedding," Maia said, as she studied her reflection in the large cheval looking glass. The girls were on the top floor of the hotel, where Minerva's studio had been turned into a temporary dressing room so they could all get ready together. While Lillian fussed around making sure her creations were perfect, two young hotel maids fashioned the girls' hair into a complicated series of loops and soft curls, each one different from the other.

"I'm not sure it bothers him all that much," Selene said. "They disowned him years ago because he made his living as a gambler. Which didn't stop them from accepting the money he sent home on a regular basis."

The girls exchanged a sober look among themselves. Imagine turning your back on your own blood.

"Good thing he has us as his family now," Selene said.

"As will TJ, once you two exchange vows," Minerva said to Chandra. "Although it's hard to imagine anything would prevent his father from being here when you two marry.

They seemed quite close. At least, I got that impression watching them on stage together."

"It's been just the two of them almost forever," Chandra said. "TJ settled here to give his father an easier life. But I guess life on the road is all his father knows."

"Was his father angry TJ wouldn't go with him?" asked Maia.

"I don't think so. Honestly, we've been too busy with the theater to speak about much else." She didn't miss the puzzled look from her sisters. Who could blame them. For someone who was supposedly madly in love, she was shockingly ignorant about TJ's background.

"Did you ever find out why he'd been in jail?" This from Selene.

"It was a case of mistaken identity, soon put to rights. He was released with an apology," she added vaguely, not sure how true that was but it sounded good, like TJ was firmly in the right. She was quite certain the story he'd shared about the married woman and her husband was for her ears only.

"There you are, miss." The young maid set aside the hot iron she had been using to coax Chandra's hair to behave. Lillian helped her into her gown, then tugged and fussed with flounces and ruffles. Finally, she nodded and stepped back. Chandra turned and studied her reflection. The claret silk taffeta was indeed a flattering color against her pale skin and dark hair. The fitted jacket followed the lines of the dress's nipped in waist and made her figure appear more voluptuous than it was, while the gathered detailing near the hem made her appear taller. Lillian stood anxiously to one side, obviously waiting for praise.

"Very nice," Chandra said with a little nod, careful not to dislodge her curls. The entire production seemed like a lot of bother for a dress she'd only wear for a few hours.

Perhaps she could write it into a play at some point. Get more wear out of it.

Selene was the last one to be helped into her gown, an engineering feat of white satin, overlaid with layers of fine lace edged in pearls. Chandra could already see the long train was going to be a liability. When she got married—

Where had that thought come from? She had no intention of marrying.

Finally they were all ready. Hanging tightly to the railing, Chandra followed her sisters to where Afi paced below, frowning at his timepiece. As she reached the lobby, Flo handed her a nosegay of fresh flowers that Afi had imported from heaven only knew where. The top button hole of his formal dress coat with tails sported a white rose bud.

"There you are!" he said in a relieved tone of voice. "Poor old Beckett is probably starting to think you changed your mind."

Did Afi look nervous? Wasn't this the day he'd been waiting for? The first of his charges being passed into the safekeeping of some other man.

Selene laughed. "He knows better. Besides, isn't it the bride's privilege to be late?"

Afi harumphed as he took Selene's arm. "My lovely Carolyn would never have kept me on tenterhooks at the altar."

Chandra exchanged an amused look with the others. "Not even to test your patience, just a little," she teased.

Outside, Smithy had the coach polished and waiting. Chandra piled in last. She loathed being squished in the middle, a constant her entire childhood. Sandwiched between two older sisters who were tasked with looking after her.

It was a breathtaking September day, blue sky and

golden sunshine backgrounding the deciduous trees tinged with red and gold, nestled between the towering evergreens. The lake glimmered a short distance away, its turquoise waters so still they barely kissed the rocky shore.

"It's so beautiful here," Selene said, patting Afi on the hand closest. "Thank you for settling us here."

Afi cleared his throat, as if his tie was suddenly too tight. "I might have brought you here. I've yet to see you settled." He cracked a forced smile. "But today is a good start."

Chandra felt all eyes on her, as if anticipating some comment about her and TJ. She turned to stare out the window, avoiding any probing looks. Before long they pulled up in front of St. Patrick's church. It was a simple wood structure, white with a front steeple crowned by a plain wooden cross. Several rows of headstones were visible on the grassy slope behind it. The church had been erected by Afi when the town was first established. Today, it was sure to be standing room only.

In the vestibule, the girls congregated next to Afi. The organist played a melancholy hymn that sounded vaguely familiar. Chandra tiptoed to the doorway and peeked out. The pews were packed, guests sitting shoulder to shoulder. Those not lucky enough to have seats stood around the sides of the church, huddled next to the stations of the cross. At the altar, next to the minister, Beckett stood straight and tall alongside his groomsmen.

She didn't spare a second glance to her soon-to-be brother-in-law. Instead, her eyes skipped over to TJ. How handsome he looked. Broad shoulders tapered to narrow hips beneath the tails of his formal, dove gray morning suit. He matched Beckett and Bolton in height and towered over the other groomsman, Antoine someone. She'd met him for the first time last night at the rehearsal and dinner afterwards, and knew precious little about him except he was Beckett's righthand man at the emporium.

Behind her, Selene gave a little gasp. She turned to see the back of Selene as she fled out the door. Maia and Minerva stood woodenly, glaring at Afi, who looked ashen. Chandra bolted after her sister, catching up with her at the carriage. "What is it? What happened?"

Selene's eyes were brimming with unshed tears.

"Did you know?"

"Know what?" She glanced over her shoulder toward the church, signaling the other girls to stay back.

"Afi. He intended all along for Beckett and I to make a match. He deliberately manipulated us to be together constantly at the emporium."

"Who cares?"

"Fine for you," Selene said bitterly. "You can rest assured Afi didn't handpick TJ as your intended. Here I thought we were modern women, making our own way, making choices. And all that time, behind the scenes—" Her sob rose to a low wail.

"Ssshhh. Today is not a day for tears," she said, watching a lone tear balance on the tip of Selene's lashes. She gave her sister an awkward hug, careful not to wrinkle their gowns or muss their hair. "We are everything you just said. Independent women at the end of the nineteenth century. Fortunate to see females finally getting the power due them. You, sister-dearest, were just lucky enough to meet a man with the same goals and interests. One whose heart joined with yours. Who cares how he came to be in your life?"

Selene gave her a suspicious look. "You sound like you know how it feels to be in love."

"It happened much faster for me," she said, glibly. "But the end result is the same. We have both chosen men who will cheer us on in our endeavors, not hold us back."

"That's true, isn't it." Selene brightened. Her tears rescinded before they spilled onto her cheeks and smeared her face powder.

"Now come on," Chandra said, taking her arm. "Put the poor man out of his misery. Last I peeked in, he was pacing a hole in the carpet."

"Beckett doesn't pace."

"He might if he thought you'd changed your mind."

Selene straightened and transferred her bouquet to her other hand. With her free hand, she took Chandra's and squeezed. "You're right. I love him. I'm marrying him. That's all that matters." Head high, back straight she marched forward. Behind her, Chandra blew out a breath of relief. Afi's constant interference would be the death of her. Thank goodness he'd stepped away from the theater, leaving her and TJ free to make their own decisions.

Afi watched from the first pew, a proud smile on his weathered features as Selene and Beckett recited their vows and exchanged rings. At least one of them was making their grandfather proud.

As the ceremony concluded, the organist played "The Wedding March". She linked her arm through TJ's as they followed Minerva and Antoine. Ahead of those two were Maia and Bolton, in the wake of the bride and groom. Their party flowed from the altar, down the center aisle and outside.

A rustling surge sounded behind them as the guests

prepared to follow the newlyweds outside. At the bottom of the steps, she and TJ moved to one side, out of the crush headed for the bride and groom. She smiled at the crudely lettered 'Just Married' sign on the back of the bride and groom's carriage, trailed by several strands of rope, each with an empty tin can attached to one end.

"There you are!" Afi bore down on them, the annoying Adria Markle hovering nearby. That woman was always trying to pretend she was part of their family. "Do you two mind going ahead to the hotel to check that everything is under control? I'll stay here with the others until the hired carriages arrive."

"Benjamin, I can go if you like," Adria said.

Chandra gritted her teeth. "No need. TJ and I will go right now."

"Take the family rig," Afi said, waving his arm. "The other carriages will be here shortly."

She shot TJ an amused look. "Take the bride's conveyance? Won't Selene be miffed?"

Afi snorted. "You'll be doing her a favor. I swear Smithy must be getting eccentric in his old age with that sign."

TJ helped her in. They were barely settled when the driver started off with a jolt that threw her against TJ in a not unpleasant way. "I've never seen Afi in such a tizzy," she said as she straightened. Her leg snugged close to TJ's, sending tingling ripples up and down her limbs to her midsection. Her chest tightened and her heart felt like it skipped a beat. She couldn't tear her eyes from his face.

"Understandable. It's not every day he walks one of you down the aisle."

"Funny to see him discombobulated, after his constant grumblings about wanting nothing more than to see us all married off."

"What happens next?" TJ stretched both arms along the seatback. The one closest to her brushed her back and shoulders in a lingering fashion. His cheeky smile told her it was deliberate. When he stroked the back of her neck, a syrupy warmth melted through her. Any attempt at conversation was an effort.

"Have you never been to a wedding?" She bit her lip the second the words left her mouth. He'd told her he and his father had been on the move constantly. Not exactly conducive to making friends and attending weddings and parties.

As he continued to watch her, a lazy smile lifting his lips, something inside her curled and stretched, forcing her to shift. She needed to be closer to him. To feel his hard length pressed against her, his lips atop hers.

"TJ—" His name on her lips was a plea, a surrender.

"Chandra—" His breath was warm against her brow as he drew her to him.

Their mouths met and fused, hot and hungry. Her nosegay fell, unheeded, to the floor of the carriage. Her hands burrowed beneath his jacket, while his mouth plundered hers. She felt his heart pound, keeping time with the racing pulse of hers. His hands molded the soft curves of her bosom causing a delicious warmth to spill through her and settle in her nether regions. She squirmed against him, tried to get closer, to feel all of him, chafing at the layers of clothing between them.

She had his tie off and two buttons of his shirt open before he pushed her voluminous skirt aside. One hand inched up the inside of her leg. Past her stockings and her petticoat to the strip of bare skin riding her stocking edge.

She held her breath. The needful juncture at the top of her legs grew damp, throbbing with need.

TJ disentangled himself from her and dropped to his knees on the floor of the carriage. His eyes glittered with intent as he pushed her legs apart and positioned his mouth where his hand had been. Pressing moist kisses to the soft skin of her inner thigh. He pulled back and speared her with his gaze. His eyes glittered with approval.

"No fancy knickers for m'lady?"

She flushed. Did men and women speak about just matters? "They felt too bulky beneath my gown."

"And would have been sorely in my way."

He returned to his ministrations. She felt his breath seconds before the tip of his tongue found her innermost secrets.

"Oh!" She gasped softly at the lap of his tongue against her as she threaded her fingers through the silky strands of his hair. She'd had no idea—

As he continued his ministrations, inner ripples built to an unbearable pitch. That building eruption she experienced once before continued to build before it abruptly crested, a sensation that left her weak and trembling. TJ took her in his arms and kissed her gently on the lips. He tasted different.

She ran a finger wonderingly over his lips. "Is this the way I taste?"

He laughed aloud. "You minx. You delight and beguile me in ways you have no idea."

As sanity slowly returned, she sat up, smoothed her gown and looked out the carriage window. "We should have been at the hotel before now." Sensual delights receded as she gripped his hand. "None of our surroundings look familiar."

To her relief, TJ took charge, leaning out the window and calling to Smithy. "I say, are we lost?"

She couldn't make out the driver's response. But there was no mistaking his troubled look as he sat back down.

"What's wrong?"

"I don't know who's got the reins, but it's not the regular driver."

CHAPTER 15

"If that isn't typical of our flighty younger sister," Selene fumed to Bolton and the others who had arrived from the church just behind her and Beckett. "Afi sent her on ahead, yet she's nowhere to be found. Luckily, Flo is more reliable." Hotel staff carrying trays of liquid refreshments circulated among the wedding guests gathered in the lobby.

Bolton stepped forward and lowered his voice. "You're sure she's not here?"

"Positive. None of the staff has seen her, and the family carriage is not in the drive."

"Where could she have gone?" Maia's brow was wrinkled with concern.

"I don't know and I don't care. But I'm not about to let her ruin my wedding day or steal all the attention, if that's what she's about."

Bolton saw Minerva exchange an anxious look with Maia. "I can't believe she would just take off."

"Nor I." Maia sent Bolton a pleading look. "We need to stay with Selene and keep her calm. Do you think you and a couple of men you trust could make a few discreet inquiries among the guests? And don't say anything to Afi, please. He's wound up like a top as it is."

Just then the minister approached Maia and Bolton. "Sorry to intrude, but there's something you need to know."

"What is it?"

The cleric bobbed his head toward the front door. Maia and Bolton exchanged a look as they followed the man. Seated on the stone wall edging the driveway, out of sight from the hotel's front entrance, Smithy, the family's driver, was surrounded by a few wedding guests.

He gave Maia an apologetic look. "Sorry, miss. I was securing the last of the tin cans on the back of the carriage when someone smote me from behind. Knocked me out cold. I came to in the cemetery out back of the church. Near-bouts everyone was gone except these kind folk who fetched me here."

Maia's gaze flew to Bolton. "Chandra didn't simply take off. She was kidnapped."

Lila joined the group, sliding her hand into Bolton's. "What's happened? Is there anything I can do to help?"

Bolton gave her a quick kiss. "Stay and reassure Selene that all is under control. I'll round up a few capable men and see if we can follow the carriage tracks. Unfortunately, whoever made off with Chandra and TJ has a healthy lead."

CHANDRA LOOKED at TJ with wide eyes. "What should we do?"

"You stay put. Let me handle this." He stood, removed his jacket and grabbed his tie, which Chandra had ripped from his throat earlier. He wound it around his right hand. He missed the compact Derringer he'd started carrying since he was attacked, but a wedding hadn't seemed an event where it might be needed.

Silently he slid open the hatch in the roof of the carriage. With a mighty heave he pulled himself up and tumbled onto the roof. The carriage was traveling at breakneck speed through a part of the country he'd not seen before, ascending into the mountains. Nothing was in sight except trees lining a narrow roadway barely wide enough for the carriage.

Grasping the luggage racks for balance, he inched his way forward until he was directly behind the driver. Just before he struck, the man turned as if sensing his presence. Murder shone from maniacal eyes, visible beneath his black eye mask.

Pulling hard on the reins before he released them, he lunged for TJ. The carriage rocked from side to side as the horses slowed, feeling the sudden absence of a driver's hand. The other man was big, lumbering and missed his target as TJ rolled to one side then the other, managing to kick the fellow in the face as he did.

The driver gave his head a shake as if his gaze was blurred and TJ took advantage to swing behind him, the tie stretched between both hands. Swiftly, dodging the other's man's clumsy blow that glanced off one shoulder, he looped the tie around his opponent's neck and pulled tight.

The man's hands clawed at his throat, attempting to loosen the tie. TJ braced himself with his feet and wound the makeshift weapon tighter. It wouldn't take long until the man's windpipe collapsed. Beneath them, the carriage continued to slow.

At last, with one final jerk, his opponent collapsed against him, knocking him from the carriage. He landed heavily, stumbled to his feet and started to run. Before he could catch up to the transport, he saw Chandra's head pop out, followed by the rest of her, crawling across the carriage roof to the driver's seat. She must have picked up the reins. He heard her whistle to the horses. Obviously confused by what had happened, they slowed to a stop.

Chandra clambered down, gave the horses a reassuring pat, then turned and started to run toward him. He increased his pace and met her halfway. They flew into each other's arms and clung tightly. It was several minutes before either spoke. And then they both spoke at the same time, the words rushing out.

"Are you all right—?"

"That was totally foolhardy—"

"You could have been killed—"

"Is he dead?"

TJ silenced her with a kiss. "We'll talk about this later. Right now we need to get back. Do you have any idea where we are?"

Chandra glanced around, still clinging to him as if she'd never let go. "Not a clue. The horses are smart though. Smithy trained them himself. They'll get us back safely." She inclined her head to where the dead driver lay atop the coach. "What about him?"

"I'll tie him on so he doesn't fall off. If we're lucky, someone knows who he is and what he was up to."

ON THEIR WAY BACK, it was a relief to run into Bolton and a few others, and turn the deceased assailant over for him to deal with.

"We'll talk about all this later," Bolton said as he took

charge of the dead man. "Right now, you need to get back to the wedding. Pretend everything is fine."

They arrived to find the wedding reception in full swing, and took a few minutes to make themselves presentable before joining the festivities. Selene and Beckett sat at a head table, two conspicuously empty places on the end.

She stood next to TJ at the back of the ballroom watching a few guests navigate the dance floor, amazed that no one here had the slightest idea what they'd just been through. A group of local musicians played their instruments in one corner. She looked from the dancers to TJ, a little rumpled but still handsome. Not to mention brave. It was thanks to him she was standing here at all.

"Do you think the kidnapper intended to grab the bride and groom and got us by mistake?"

"It's a strong possibility, since we were in the coach with the Just Married sign."

"Selene would have freaked right out. I doubt Beckett would have been as quick to secure their release as you were ours." She shuddered. "We likely saved my sister from a potentially nasty situation and she doesn't even know."

"I'm sure she'll thank you once she knows what happened."

She gave a humorless laugh. "Not Selene. She'll find some way to make it all my fault."

He gave his head a rueful shake. "Be grateful for what you have. A family who loves and supports you." He squeezed her shoulder. "Speaking of family, I see your grandfather summoning you from across the room. You'd better go appease him."

"Not without you," she said. "He's more likely to believe the story of what happened from your mouth than mine."

Keeping a firm hold of TJ, she crossed the ballroom to

where Afi sat at a prominent table. She was pleased the irritating widow Markle wasn't hanging at his side making a pest of herself.

"Where have you been?" Afi snapped. "Your sister was fit to be tied."

She shot TJ a look. "I guess no one told you we were kidnapped." She plunked herself into an empty chair next to her grandfather. TJ stood behind her. She could have kissed him for the supportive way he rested one hand on her shoulder.

"You were what?" Afi sputtered. His face turned red, whether from anger or affront she had no idea. "Where is the responsible party? I'll see them strung up and—"

"TJ took care of him," she said. "We turned his body over to Bolton. He'll send someone he trusts to deliver it to the sheriff at White Sulphur Springs."

Afi's hand shook slightly as he picked up his whisky glass and took a healthy slug. "We can't count on Dodds to get to the bottom of things. He has his hands full in his own town." He raised his piercing gaze. "You're both all right?"

She patted TJ's hand where it lay on her shoulder. "TJ was very brave. He risked his own life to keep me safe."

Afi gave TJ a long look. "I'm sorry if I misjudged you, son. I took you for an opportunist, looking for the easy road to a comfortable life. Seeing what you've done, your work transforming the warehouse, plus saving my granddaughter. I couldn't ask for a better addition to our family."

TJ shot her an accusing look, his displeasure obvious at continuing to deceive the old man. "Thank you, sir. I hope you continue to feel that way." Everything he didn't say hung unspoken between him and her, leaving a hollow feeling in her midsection.

Yes, Afi would be disappointed with her when she left

for the bright lights out East. She just hoped he loved her enough to one day understand why she did it. She looked from her grandfather to TJ. It would be her who incurred Afi's disapproval, not TJ. No, her jilted fiancé would come off like a hero for having put up with her selfish ways this long.

She could hear her sisters already. How she only thought of herself, as usual. Consoling TJ, berating her actions. Who knew? Perhaps after a suitable period of time passed, he'd find solace in the company of either Maia or Minerva. After all he'd already won a stamp of approval from Afi. Had earned his place in Silver Springs Junction and her family.

She frowned, not much liking for the idea of TJ with one of her sisters. Giving them the same amazing experience as he did her in the carriage. Making someone else feel the same tingles of desire whenever she laid eyes on him.

"I'm a foolish, stubborn old man." Afi spoke more to himself than to her or TJ. "Thinking I know best. Thinking I have it all figured out. I should have listened. The Mayor and Dodds both warned me, told me the town needs a full-time lawman. How arrogant to believe I could create a town where nothing bad ever happened."

It wasn't like Afi to sound down on himself. "It's hardly your fault, Afi. As the town grows, it's bound to attract a few unscrupulous characters. This is the first serious incident." Which wasn't exactly true. They'd almost lost Beckett earlier. Afi was right to be concerned.

Afi ignored her to direct his question to TJ. "What do you think? Any chance the responsible parties were after you, and not targeting Chandra or Selene to get to me?"

"It's possible I've made a few enemies along the way," TJ said. "But it's unlikely any of them followed me here. Or had any way of knowing I'd be in that carriage."

"Maybe the parties responsible were after Beckett," she said. "It could be something as trivial as a poor loser from the emporium."

"Unfortunately, we'll never know the kidnapper's motivation," TJ said. "Not unless he had an accomplice or two who accidentally slip up and show their hand."

Afi made a shooing gesture with his hands. "I'm keeping you young people from a party. And if I'm not mistaken the bride is shooting me daggers for it. Go have something to eat and enjoy the music. Try and forget about what happened."

One look at TJ told her he was as unlikely to forget the incident as she was.

CHAPTER 16

Victoria tapped Chandra gently on the top of her hand where it rested between them on the settee.

"You're ready, you know. More than ready in my estimation. Give you a stage and your audience will be enthralled, perched on the edge of their seats so as not to miss a word or a gesture."

"I've had a wonderful teacher," she said. "I just wish you would let me pay you for your time and expertise."

Victoria sat back and picked up her tea cup. "Nonsense. I've enjoyed your visits and our time together more than you will ever know. To see you flourish under my tutelage is payment enough."

"Is it forward of me to ask you to come and watch me one night? I know it's a journey, but it's not far by train. I can arrange a room at the hotel for you and your husband after the show."

"Nothing would give me more pleasure. Do you have a firm date for your debut?"

"Not yet," she said. Every time she broached the topic TJ was more evasive than ever. It's true she'd left him to arrange which performers would grace their stage, but she sensed he had little confidence in her ability to hold her own in a theater full of patrons. "We have a firm opening date, as well as the early acts lined up, but TJ appears to have his own agenda."

"Sounds like a man. The own agenda part, I mean."

"Truly." She pursed her lips, opened her mouth to speak, then closed it abruptly.

As usual, Victoria didn't miss a thing. "What else is on your mind? Other than me attending your debut performance."

"It's, uh— " She looked down to where she had twisted the dainty tea napkin into a near knot in her lap. "Before you were married to Mr. Danford did you have— did you take— I mean the theater life was different from most others, was it not?"

"Did I take a lover?" Victoria asked, with a twinkle in her eye.

"That's what I wondered, yes," she said, a warm flush creeping up her neck to her cheeks. Why was this so hard? Women across the country were gaining ground every day, through politics, land ownership, ability to divorce. They were no longer mere chattel, yet she was unable to discuss the intimacies of marriage with her one married sister.

"I see you wear a man's betrothal ring," Victoria said. "Are you curious what your wedding night might be like?"

"Not at all," she said. "I have no intention of marrying, ever." She twisted the ring on her finger. "This is just to appease my grandfather. But I—" She cleared her throat. "I've recently discovered there are pleasurable ways to experience intimacy without, you know, without—"

"Without intercourse," Victoria said.

"That's right," she murmured.

"Well, aren't you a lucky young lady. And might I ask if this is something you discovered on your own? Or with the aid of your young man?"

Her face felt like it was burning. "He and I. We were— That is he, uh—"

"Knows kissing is not an action reserved solely for the lips?" Victoria suggested.

"Exactly."

Her friend's smile broadened. "Was there a question in all this?"

"I just wondered. For him. Might he achieve a similar satisfaction if I were to kiss him on, you know, more intimate areas of his body?"

"Certainly the satisfaction you experienced with your young man can be shared equally," Victoria said. "In fact, some couples prefer it to a more traditional coupling. Or as a way to enjoy each other while ensuring no offspring result from the liaison."

"Oh." She sat back so suddenly she bounced forward again, off the settee's rear cushion. "I never even considered—"

"A man who puts a woman's pleasure and well-being ahead of his own is a rare find, my dear. I would hang onto this fellow if I were you."

TJ PERUSED CRAWFORD'S STUDY. One entire wall was filled floor to ceiling with shelves of books that didn't appear to have ever been opened. What he wouldn't give to have a personal library at his disposal. The far wall held dozens of framed sketches. He recognized early renditions of the railway station, the hotel, the gambling emporium and other local buildings, while others were unfamiliar. Perhaps from different towns Crawford played a part in helping to establish.

He had no idea why he had been summoned. Crawford had sent a houseman to the theater with a request to join him at the hotel at his earliest convenience. He'd been shown to the study to find a man wearing a sheriff's badge next to Bolton Edge. Bolton introduced him to sheriff Dodds from White Sulphur Springs. Just then the patriarch joined them and took a seat behind his desk.

"Sorry to keep you waiting, gentlemen. I presume you've all met?" TJ gave a brief nod before his gaze shifted from man to man. Why was he here?

"Any update on the low-life who kidnapped my grand-daughter?" Crawford directed his question to the sheriff.

Dodds pursed his lips. "I told you, these things take time. Dead men don't talk much. And neither do their friends."

"Bolton, anything through your channels?"

"As far as I've been able to find out, there was no price on the kidnapper's head."

Crawford looked TJ's way. "Too bad you had to snuff him. We might never find out who he was working for."

He tensed. "All due respect, sir. Chandra's life was in danger. The coach was traveling at breakneck speed. I didn't have the opportunity to overpower him and tie him up all tidy so he could be delivered to the law."

"I know. I know," Crawford said. "And I'm grateful for your quick action. I just hate not knowing the intent. Who, exactly the varmint was after. And why."

Maybe Crawford thought he knew more than he was saying. That's why he'd been summoned.

"We might know more if you'd taken my suggestion to have a dedicated lawman in town." This from Dodds.

"Point well taken. If it's all right with your office, I'm going to ask that your higher-ups appoint Bolton as acting sheriff. Till we can have a proper election. The mayor thinks it's a good idea."

Bolton straightened. "Were you going to consult me on this latest scheme of yours?"

Crawford shrugged. "Can't think of anyone better. Your wife has settled in here nicely. Being married is hardly conducive to your previous line of work."

He'd assumed Bolton worked for Crawford. But maybe not. Had he made a mistake giving the man the cache of jewelry he'd found planted among his things?

"One of these days, Crawford, you might not get everything your way like you're accustomed to."

So that's where Chandra gets it!

Crawford's gaze grew steely on Bolton. "I lost my wife. I lost my daughter. I wouldn't call that having the gods smiling on me, would you?"

Bolton nodded. "Sorry. I spoke without thinking."

Crawford turned to Dodds. "Well?"

"I'll look into it." Dodds rose. "Glad to see you finally come to your senses, Crawford. You should get the paperwork in the next few days. Somehow, I expect the election will be more of a formality than anything."

Still not sure why he'd been included, TJ followed the example of the other men who rose to shake hands with Dodds. He remained standing, prepared to also take his leave as Crawford walked the sheriff to the door.

"Sit down, Dirks," Crawford said. "Got a couple of things to discuss with you still." He closed the door behind Dodds and returned to his desk. "Bolton? You want to bring him up to date?"

"I've been following up with the jewelry you found planted in your belongings. Turns out several of the items were pieces that went missing in the hotel." TJ opened his mouth, then closed it when Bolton held up a hand. "Don't worry, no one thinks you were responsible. The thefts happened long before you arrived in town."

He breathed a sigh of relief. He'd suspected as much, but one never knew what conclusions might be drawn. Especially given his history.

"The remainder of the jewelry is proving a little harder to trace. And difficult to prove you didn't lift them, then have a sudden attack of conscience."

"Other than my word," he said flatly. He looked from one man to the other. "I had nothing to do with the robbery that was pinned on me before, but my word at the time was worthless."

"No one's accusing you of anything," Bolton said. "Been a lot of newcomers to the area lately. I just want you to stay on your guard. And let me know if you see anything that appears suspicious. Or anyone who looks familiar that you may have had a run-in with before."

CHANDRA THREW down the final copy of the theater's opening acts. She tracked down TJ in one of the theater's dressing rooms, hunched over while he made some adjustments to a stool. Temporarily distracted, she watched his large capable hands tackle the task, smiling as she recalled him pushing aside the hem of her bridesmaid dress, his fingers cool against her heated flesh.

Belatedly she recalled why she was here. If she squinted, she could almost see herself seated in front of the mirrors at her own dressing table, perfecting her makeup and getting into character for her next performance. Once TJ stopped holding her back. She blew out an exasperated breath. Victoria had told her to hang onto him. Right now, she was more than ready to drop kick him into the river.

"I see you've still not scheduled me for next month's line-up."

TJ put down his screwdriver, rose to his full height and tipped his head sideways. "Let's just see how things go with the more established acts coming through first."

"Everyone thinks I'm ready." Well, Victoria did, anyway. No one else took her endeavors seriously. No one else had any idea what she was capable of.

"You're a Crawford. Folks have a way of telling you and your family what they want to hear."

Was that true? Could Victoria be placating her?

She pounded the dressing table with her fist. "We had a deal. You get to run the theater. I get to build my career. Why are you so determined to stand in my way?" Her voice rose accusingly. "Or is it that you don't want me to succeed? Afraid if I leave Afi will give you your marching orders and reclaim the building. Use it for his own purposes. Leaving you high and dry."

"That's not it."

"Then what *is it*?"

TJ reached across the table, and placed his hand atop hers. "I care about you, Chandra. I'd hate to see you become hurt or disillusioned. Life on the stage, even what little I've experienced, is hard. And full of disappointments."

"Does this have anything to do with your mother? Her running off when you were young?"

He pressed his lips into a thin line. "One thing has nothing to do with the other."

Which meant it was time to practice her feminine wiles.

She rounded the table and insinuated her body tightly against his, pinning him to the wall. His eyes narrowed, guarded. She tipped her head back, thrust out her bosom, and gave him what she hoped was a provocative smile. She glanced sideways in the mirror. Definitely provocative. She heard his raggedly indrawn breath. Felt him flinch when she trailed her fingers up his exposed forearm, ruffling the dark hair peppering his skin.

"There are empty nights in the schedule. Why are you so against me making my stage debut?"

"The theater needs to prove itself. It's important we take time to gauge the audience, make sure their expectations are met. That's how word will spread."

"And you don't think I'm good enough? Is that it?" Boldly she angled one leg between his. She could feel his body heat through the layers of clothing that separated them. A rush of pleasure pulsed through her as she remembered their intimate encounter in the carriage.

Recalling Victoria's words, she slid her fingers just inside the waistband of his trousers. "That day in the carriage. The amazing things you made me feel. I want to make you feel the same way. There is much we can do for each other. Give to each other."

She swayed forward, one hand on the front of his trousers, the other arm looped around his neck, pulling him down for her kiss. She felt his brief hesitation before he crushed her to him, his hungry lips feeding from hers. She moaned as his hands molded her bosom, kneading her nipples into fiery pleasure points that sent molten lava to her nether regions.

This was wrong!

She was supposed to be seducing *him*.

She walked him sideways along the wall to the corner settee where it didn't take much effort to push him onto his back. He raised himself onto his elbows and lay there, legs splayed in a suggestive way. Watching her. Waiting to see what she did next.

If only she knew! She ought to have gleaned more information from Victoria.

When in doubt— She pulled the pins from her hair and gave her head a shake, feeling the heavy strands tumble about her shoulders and down her back. Better. She felt wicked. Wanton. She knelt at his side and reached for the fastening on his trousers.

His hand manacled her wrist, arresting her movements. He sat up.

"I believe you've made your point."

"What point is that?" She sat back on her heels, confused. This was not the way things were supposed to play out.

"That you'll do anything to get what you want. Lie to your grandfather. Make a deal with Callan. Seduce me. All in the name of your ambitions."

"I never deceived you. I made my intentions known from the first." She rose as she spoke, at a loss what to do next. He rose as well. Towered over her in a way that made her feel ineffectual. She dug into her repertoire of fictional stage characters, raised herself on tiptoe and looked him in the eye. "You understood from the start where we stand."

"Then things happen along the way. Isn't that right? The best laid plans and all that—"

"Th—things? What sort of things?"

His hand clasped the back of her neck, fingers tangled in

the mane of loose hair. She shivered at the intensity of his look. His touch.

He drew her close. His kiss sparked lightning through her limbs, frantic and hot, then slow and melting. Somehow, she wound up on the settee with him stretched atop her. His leg nested between hers, his knee pressing suggestively on that throbbing inner sanctum. He was throbbing as well. She could feel him pulsing against her leg.

Her hips shimmied in an effort to get closer, seeking a relief that only he could bring. Using his elbows for leverage, he raised his upper body and cupped her face in his hands before running his hands through her hair, probing her scalp, making her shiver in anticipation.

His grin was smug. Knowing. "You enjoyed out little interlude, didn't you?"

She nodded. Words were unnecessary. The air crackled as their gazes held. Tension continued to building in her limbs.

"And you planned to seduce me. To bring me around to your way of thinking."

She toyed with the buttons fronting his shirt. "You brought me such satisfaction. I felt a mutual exchange was in order."

"Did you now?" His smile was wolfish.

"I did."

"And nothing in it for you? A simple, selfless act."

"That's right." She reached again for the front fastening of his trousers.

He pushed her hand away, tucked it in his and trapped it between them. She blinked in confusion as he rolled off her and onto his feet where he stood looking down at her. Was that disappointment in his eyes?

"I've been seduced and pleasured by women far more

skilled in the act. The end result was always the same. I felt used. I will not be toyed with or manipulated. Save your longing sighs and pent-up sexual energy for someone else. Someone who doesn't mind being a means to an end."

She pushed herself to a sitting position. "I thought we were talking about a mutual benefit. You and I each getting what we want."

"We want totally different things, Chandra. And a quick coupling won't change that."

Parting shot delivered, he strolled from the room.

"Ack," she fumed, wishing she had something to throw. As she stared at the empty doorway, inspiration struck. A different way to bring TJ around.

TJ WALKED through an aisle of the empty theater, envisioning it with the seats full of excited theatergoers. Opening night loomed on the horizon with nearly all tickets spoken for, thanks in part to his hobo friends who spread the word near and far in their travels. The rest stemmed from Callan's influence with the press.

Chandra had been keeping her distance, and he wasn't sure what had annoyed her the most. Him rejecting her overtures in the dressing room that day, or the fact that he hadn't included her in the first month's schedule. She was so vibrant and spirited and alive; she'd brought sunlight into his dark days. Her passion was infectious. Fear of failure wasn't in her vocabulary, yet it was something he wrestled with every single day. It wasn't just failure. It was letting down those around you who depended on you. Not meeting their expectations.

He swung toward the sound of the outside door opening. A shadowy figured stood in the entrance. His heart lurched thinking it was Chandra, then realized it was Ryder Lyon. Even though Lyon worked for Callan, who had put up the funds for the theater, TJ didn't trust the man. But then he didn't trust many. Especially reporters. They'd been his worst enemy when he was trying to prove his innocence over his lover's missing jewelry. He still got a knot in his gut, worried it was happening all over again. Someone out to frame him for the jewel thefts.

"Callan said I should come beg a tour," Lyon said. "He's asked me to write a short series, some teasing tidbit he can feature in the papers each day until the doors open."

"It's after opening night that we need the positive press," TJ said. "Hope the critics are on board."

"Is that why you're playing it safe with the line up?" Ryder asked.

"Who thinks I'm playing it safe?"

Ryder shot him a telling look.

"Is Callan worried about his investment?"

Ryder laughed and shook his head. "Callan has so many irons in so many different fires I doubt even he can keep track of them. But for some reason, this little project has captured a special place in his heart."

He personally figured Callan Douglas had a money pouch where his heart used to be, but it wasn't his place to say so. "Hard to figure him out. Or Crawford."

"Don't even waste your time trying. One minute they appear to be sworn enemies, the next it's like they're best of friends. Brothers from another mother."

"Crawford's the one who pulled his backing for here. I don't think he anticipated Callan swooping in to take his place."

"Crawford's losing his edge if he didn't see that coming. At any rate, care to give me the nickel tour?"

"All right." After all, it was better to have friends than enemies. "Let's start over here."

He led the reporter first to the spacious changing rooms, where Lyon didn't try to hide the fact that he was impressed by what he saw. "Much fancier than anything I've seen in long-established theaters."

"My father and I used to make a game of it. Improvements we'd implement if we had free license back stage."

Back in the main body of the theater, Lyon did what so many others did, turned in a circle to get the full effect. "You've pulled off an interesting feat of creating a theater-in-the round from a square building."

"Illusion is my specialty. The same way words are yours."

"Words and people," Lyon said. "Are you familiar with an actress named Victoria Danford?"

"The retired stage legend?" TJ said.

"The same," Lyon said. "One of the Crawford girls told me Chandra is trying to entice her to attend opening night. I hope she manages it. A patron of such renown would make for good press. The public is still curious about someone like her who leaves their profession while they're at the top of their game."

"I didn't know Miss Danford and Chandra were acquainted."

"I understand they've struck up quite a friendship," Lyon said.

Something in his words gave TJ pause. "Sounds like you have the ear of one of the girls."

"Minerva has been seeking my counsel regarding painters and the like. Artists who might be interested in becoming involved in next year's festival. At any rate, it would be a feather in your cap to have Miss Danford in attendance. That would help put the place on the map faster than anything else. What's through this door?"

"I keep it locked," TJ said. "It's a classroom, but the students will use the outside entrance."

"The Magic Stage," Lyon said. "Is it currently off limits?"

"I've been too busy to do much with it yet. One of these days soon I hope to have it up and running for lessons. How about I invite you around once that happens?"

"I look forward to it."

He followed Lyon to the door. "I hope I've satisfied your curiosity."

He didn't care for Lyon's calculating expression. "For the time being. By the way, I like what you've named the theater."

"That was Chandra's doing." She'd lobbied to call it Crawford and Co., her way of appeasing her grandfather and paying homage to the fact that Crawford owned the building. For his part, TJ hadn't cared enough one way or another to argue.

From the front door, he watched Lyon walk away, certain he hadn't seen the last of the man. Wondering what the reporter had really been hoping to find when he dropped in unannounced.

No sooner was he back inside than Chandra arrived. She wore a huge grin that made him instantly suspicious of her motives.

"You look like the cat that swallowed the canary."

"Making birds appear and disappear is your forte. I have something to show you."

Best he humor her. "What might that be?"

"It's just out here." She had hold of his arm and was

tugging him through the door. The area out front was empty. He turned to her, puzzled. "I don't see—"

She startled him by placing her hands over his eyes and guiding him away from the theater before she turned him around and lowered her hands. "Tah-duh!"

His jaw dropped. Directly over the double wide front doors, hung a freshly-painted sign. Simple but striking. *The Ophelia*. In smaller letters below, *Established 1896*.

A lump the size of a robin's egg formed in his throat. It was several minutes before he could tear his eyes from the sign to look at her.

She watched him, eyes wide as she waited for his reaction. He swallowed thickly, but the lump remained.

"From Shakespeare," she said.

"Umm hmm." What Chandra didn't know is that Ophelia had been his mother's name.

She nodded. "It seemed fitting." She slipped her hand into his. "Much better than one more thing in this town with the Crawford name, don't you think?"

And one more subtle chip away at the barrier he'd tried to put between himself and Chandra.

CHAPTER 17

TJ paced the station platform, a doomed feeling in his gut as the train discharged its passengers. He'd been here earlier to greet the other acts, but this time no one matched the description of the last pair expected, a husband-and-wife vaudeville team. The opening act for tonight's sold-out show. Desperately, he scanned the blur of faces pushing past him. They'd advertised three unique acts. As of right now, they only had two.

Spotting a familiar face, he turned away but not soon enough. Ryder Lyon, the last person he wanted to talk to right now, was shouldering a pathway toward him, an older couple trailing in his wake. As they reached his side, he recognized the woman with him. Victoria Danford! The older gentleman must be her husband.

"Dirks. Look who I charmed into joining us tonight." Lyon was grinning ear-to-ear, almost as if he knew TJ was going to fall on his face and couldn't wait for a front row ticket.

"Miss Danford!" Manners rose to the forefront as he

bent over the woman's gloved hand and raised it to his lips. "You do our town and our little theater proud with your presence."

She blessed him with her famous smile, one that had won the hearts of theatergoers for several decades. "I believe you do exaggerate, but it's my pleasure to attend. I've so enjoyed my time with the lovely Miss Chandra and wanted to lend my support." Her eyes twinkled as she looked him over from head to toe. "Might I presume you're the lucky young man who placed that stunning emerald on Chandra's finger?" She raised a brow suggestively. "I've heard such interesting things about you."

He struggled for a response. Chandra was acquainted with Miss Danford well enough that the two of them had spoken about him?

He recovered enough to say, "I'm sure you know to take whatever Chandra says with more than one grain of salt."

Miss Danford patted his hand. "In this instance, I rather think not. Lovely to meet you, TJ."

She knew his name!

She turned and tucked one hand through the crooked elbow of the silent man in the background before Lyon led the pair to a waiting carriage. The Crawford's personal coach, no less.

Around him the platform stood mockingly empty. The train's whistle gave its mournful blast, like a knife to his middle. This was the last train expected today. And no vaudeville act. After wasting a few futile moments hoping against hope the duo would pop into sight, laughing uproariously at having tricked someone who was supposed to be a master of illusions, he returned to the theater.

The place was a hub of activity inside and out. As he

spared a quick glance at the sign above the door, a flood of emotions raced through him. Chandra was full of surprises. Not the spoiled brat he'd originally thought, but someone who knew what she wanted and refused to let anything stand in her way. Which she did in a charming, inoffensive way. Maybe it was time he tried doing things her way.

Doormen and ushers passed him. Performers herded to the changerooms to stake their territory.

"I say," yelled someone from the center of the main floor. "Who's in charge around here?"

TJ turned to face the man. "That would be me. TJ Dirks."

The older fellow, not an actor, but likely part of the crew, asked, "What's the deal with the round stage? Our set's no good for that."

"Theater in the round," TJ said. "It's one of the things that makes The Ophelia unique."

"It's not the way thing have been done."

It wasn't the first time he'd heard that same argument. Folks didn't like change. Yet giving them the same old thing they'd seen before bored them. It was one of the main challenges of the entertainment industry.

He shrugged. "You've got till tonight to figure it out." It wasn't his fault the set crew didn't read the specs he'd sent with the contract.

Grumbles of discord trailed in the man's wake. Which didn't phase him. Theater folk always found something to complain about. What was he going to do about the missing act? The men in charge of lighting were readying the lanterns and spotlights which would allow the stage to be illuminated differently for each act and give the theater a unique feel.

Although the hustle and bustle of organized confusion

was a familiar scene, it felt strange to be on the other side. Folks brushed past, apparently knowing their jobs better than he did. He was considering how he might best be useful, when in burst Chandra and Miss Danford. Did he at least look like he knew what he was doing?

"There you are TJ." Chandra's face was alight with excitement, adding to the sinking inside his stomach. She had no idea that The Ophelia's opening night was about to go down in history as a dismal failure. "I insisted Miss Danford come see our pride and joy before it's stuffed to the rafters with noisy patrons." She flung her arms wide as if embracing the theater. "Isn't it even more amazing than I described? And it was all TJ's idea. A theater in the round. Walls that look like the inside of a tent are only one illusion. One of many."

Miss Danford gave him a wide smile of approval that he wished would offset the churning in his gut.

"I'm delighted to see it with my own eyes. What a triumph. It's almost enough to tempt me back to the bright lights."

He widened his eyes. Could salvation be right in front of him? "Would you? Possibly? Tonight?"

He ignored Chandra plucking at his arm, asking, "TJ, whatever do you mean? What's wrong?" His eyes were riveted on Miss Danford.

"I second Chandra's query. Why would you even suggest such a thing?"

He blew out a breath. "The opening act has failed to arrive." He looked around. "Soon we shall have a theater full of disgruntled patrons who have paid to see three different performances and are only granted two."

The women exchange a glance. Miss Danford inclined

her head at Chandra. "Looks like your debut could be earlier than you anticipated, my dear."

Chandra blanched. "Oh, no. I'm not prepared. It's too short of notice."

"Nonsense. You're as prepared as you'll ever be. Your skit with the *soubrette* and the lady of the manor is nothing short of brilliant."

"You really think so?"

He interrupted. "*Soubrette*?" He was familiar with the term but his mind had suddenly gone blank.

Chandra's expression brightened. She glanced at her timepiece. "I'll need to gather some props and costume pieces." She turned to him. "One of the other acts will have to go on first. I'll perform after them. The strongest act should close the show. That's what people will remember and talk about. The last act sells the next show. Isn't that what they say?" She turned to Miss Danford for clarification.

"Just because they say it, doesn't always mean it's true," the retired actress said. "Come. I will help you prepare."

The two left in a whirlwind, leaving him to deal with an excess of emotions warring for supremacy. He ought to be grateful to Chandra for stepping in. Instead, he was angry and disappointed, mostly with himself. His first foray at a 'normal' life was proving a dismal failure. What made him think he was cut out to stay in one place, let alone take on something so unpredictable as dealing with theater folk? He never should have listened to Chandra in the first place.

HOURS later he set aside those warring emotions. The mezzanine near his living quarters gave him a clear view of the stage and theater. The future looked less bleak as the theater began to fill up with patrons. Men, women, and children filtered in, stopping to stare in amazement at their surroundings before an usher showed them to their seats. Necks craned, heads bobbed, neighbors waved to neighbors. Maybe he wasn't a total failure after all.

Once the seats were filled, the houselights dimmed. His cue to make his way to the main floor. The hum of anticipation rose from muted to a high pitch of excitement as a spotlight flicked on, circled the room and settled on him in the formal black suit he always wore on stage, complete with tails, top hat and a crisp white shirt.

The crowd grew quiet as he approached the stage, the light illuminating his way through the audience to the cleverly concealed stage steps off to one side. He strode onto the stage, something he had imagined a hundred times over in his head these past months. His stage. His theater. His creation.

He should be in his element. After all, he'd spent his entire life on one stage or another. But never as himself. Tonight was different. He had no costume. No props. No tried-and-true sleight of hand to offer.

A drum roll echoed throughout the theater. He took his place in the center of the stage, moving constantly to address the audience on all sides of him. "Ladies and gentlemen. Welcome to opening night at The Ophelia, soon to be heralded as the greatest theater in the West." He caught sight of Crawford's gleaming white head in the VIP section.

"You're witnessing more than one historic moment tonight. For it's not your imagination. The Ophelia is truly a theater-in-the-round. I promise you this untraditional approach to theater viewing will enhance, not impede, your enjoyment of tonight's acts."

He sought out the stage master's signal that all was ready. "And now, I present to you, all the way from Philadelphia, the Flying Triplets."

He exited the stage just as a trapeze was lowered from the rafters, a costumed woman aboard. The crowd stamped and whistled. The spotlight followed the other members of the act as they ran through the audience and bounded onto the stage. TJ clapped along with the watching audience as the act began. The performer and her two 'brothers' were no more triplets than he was, but they were a talented crew that kept the viewers enthralled with their trapeze work overhead and their gymnastics on stage.

As the act progressed, he was pleased to see their performance lent itself particularly well to the round stage. But just wait—

He smiled to himself. Timing was everything. He'd learned at an early age that good theater could not be rushed. Anticipation and surprise were key elements. Taking his cues from the music, he counted silently in his head. At precisely the exact moment, he sent a signal to the main stagehand, fingers crossed that all went as planned. He doubted anyone heard the faint griding of gears as the mechanism kicked in and the stage slowly started to turn.

The audience gasped in amazement. As he had anticipated, the result resembled an oversize wind-up music box coming to life. In seconds viewers were on their feet. Deafening applause rang through the theater while the performers carried on their act as if nothing out of the ordinary was going on.

Not until the stage returned to its original starting point did the audience return to their seats. All eyes remained glued to the stage and its performers, waiting for the stage to move again. Which it would at the end of the act, as the performers took their bows. Satisfied all was well, TJ headed for the changing rooms. Time to check on Chandra.

CHANDRA'S HAND shook as she picked up a sponge to smooth a layer of stage makeup, a gift from Victoria. She wished her wise friend was here now, but she'd insisted Victoria sit out front and enjoy the show. Butterflies bashed around her insides. No amount of water eased the dryness in her throat. Would she even be able to say her lines?

She threw down the greasy makeup stick and dabbed at her cheeks with a handkerchief. She'd watched the triplets rehearse. Nothing she could offer would even come close to the entertainment value of their act. She put her head in her hands in despair. She'd be booed off the stage.

When she straightened and looked to her reflection, she started. TJ stood behind her. How long had he been watching her bumbling efforts?

She tried to act nonchalant as she picked up her wig. "I heard the audience when the stage moved." His vision had impressed her from the start. To take the same mechanism that worked her windup music box to a scale not yet attempted, and have the stage turn in a full circle.

He was brilliant. Sure to succeed no matter what he took on. Unlike her. Poised to humiliate herself in front of the entire town, including family and friends.

The wig dropped from her hands to the table in front of her. "I'm sorry TJ. I can't. I just can't do this. I'm not ready. In fact," she started to stand. "I may never be ready."

He caught her hands in both of his and pulled her close. "Would you believe me if I told you that what you're feeling is completely normal?"

She made a scoffing noise. "I'm not like you. I didn't grow up on a stage. All I've had is this fanciful dream." His hands on hers felt nice. Warm. Strong. Capable. She needed what he offered. His strength. His confidence. His support.

"Don't ever let anyone tell you dreams don't come true. I didn't even know I was capable of having a dream till I met you." He released one hand to move his arm in a sweeping gesture. "You've helped me to create all this. More than I would have dared to dream about. And now—" His voice sounded choked. "Don't you see, together, there is nothing we can't achieve?"

If only she believed him. What he said and more. What if the ring on her finger, their supposed betrothal, were more than a ruse? She stared down at the ring. She'd grown used to wearing it. It felt real. Yet it, too, was only smoke and mirrors. An illusion that other people bought into.

She straightened her shoulders.

"Have them extend the intermission a little. I need to prepare."

As TJ left, she went over the skit in her mind one more time. She'd be playing two women, a *soubrette* or ladies' maid, foil to her employer, a lady to the manor born. But despite their differences in circumstances, the two were remarkably similar, which is what gave the performance its humor.

On-stage changes were simple. As the maid she wore an apron and carried a duster. As the lady of the house, she sported an elaborate hat. The set was minimal. A chair. A side table and lamp. A carpet. The humor was all in the gestures. The delivery. And her ability to play both parts convincingly.

Play to the audience; the actress's creed. She hugged the words to her as she left the dressing room and took her position. When she heard her cue, she stepped forward, blinking as her eyes adjusted to the lights. Beyond the lights ringing the stage, the audience was a faceless dark mass. Miraculously, the dryness in her throat disappeared. And just like that, she became the characters. Sophia and Mrs. Bigenbottom took over.

CHAPTER 18

"You were wonderful!"

"Amazing!"

"Stole the show!"

Her three sisters burst into the dressing room, chattering madly as they made a beeline in her direction. She caught the condescending looks that came her way from a couple of the other performers. Their message was clear. She wasn't one of them. She didn't belong here. A fact reinforced by her sisters' chatter.

"I appreciate your enthusiasm, sisters, but please don't forget to congratulate the others here. It's their reputation that brought us the audience. I was simply a last-minute fill-in."

"Last minute or not, you were brilliant," Selene said. "Afi has invited a select crew back to the hotel to celebrate your triumph. And TJ's of course."

"Oh." Chandra made eye contact in the mirror with the woman behind her. She'd heard the others talking earlier. An afterparty in the local saloon near their rooming house. She'd been hoping to be asked to join them.

When the woman turned away, she sighed. Just like that, she reverted to 'lady of the manor'. The heiress playing at a stage career.

"Give me a few minutes to finish up here," she said. "Then I'll collect TJ and head to the hotel."

Maia cocked a look. "Is he ever going to tell you what his initials stand for? I mean, why the secrecy?"

"I can only imagine it must be something truly dreadful," Selene said.

Minerva cast her a sympathetic look. "Come along you two. Leave Chandra in peace to get changed." Chandra shot her a look of gratitude. She loved her sisters, but sometimes they were a little much. Especially in a pack.

She turned to the other performers. "I know you lot don't take me seriously. And that's understandable. I'm new to all this. I need to prove myself. Just be aware I intend to do exactly that. No matter how long it takes."

One by one, she sent each of them a challenging look, only to be ignored. No one returned her gaze. She pulled on her cloak. Fine. Let them have their pathetic little party in the saloon. One day they'd look back on this and regret they weren't kinder. They'd be begging her to join them, but she'd have far better offers.

The second she stepped outside, the truth hit her. She was behaving like a spoiled brat who didn't get her own way. She needed to earn the respect of others, not expect it as her due because of who she was. She glanced toward the river and the hobo camp. She'd been too busy lately to take them any food. She must do better. Fortunate circumstances didn't make her a better person, just a luckier one.

Up ahead, she saw TJ walking toward her and her heart kicked up a beat. This was not the time to be berating herself for her shortcomings. "I hear there's a party in our honor at the hotel."

"I heard." The second he reached her side she sensed an invisible barrier between them. Didn't he know she longed for him to sweep her into his arms? Regret swept through her. Who could blame him for keeping his distance? What a shallow and selfish young woman she'd been a few short months ago.

She'd thought herself so clever. Tricking him into a false betrothal. She fingered the emerald ring beneath her gloves, comfortingly heavy on her finger. How could she let him know the ring and everything it stood for meant something to her? That he meant something to her. Her feelings for him were not just something concocted on a whim when convenient, but deep and true.

"The coachman just left with your sisters and grandfather. He said he'd be back for you shortly. I told him I'd wait."

"You were amazing tonight." She clasped his arm, remembering their moment in the dressing room. The reassurance of his hands on hers.

He gave a rueful smile. "I think that's my line to you."

"All right then. We were both amazing. Triumphant in our individual roles."

He took her hand from his arm and clasped it in his. Lowered his head; brought it near hers. Her breath caught in her throat. Was he closing in for a kiss? She preened at the approval in his eyes and his voice.

"You saved the evening. The triumph is yours."

She waved her free hand toward the theater. "This entire undertaking would never have been half as brilliant without your vision and persistence and hard work."

He bit off a laugh. "I'm not the one who bullied the mill-wright to push our order to the front of the queue."

"Well, all right," she said, pressing her lips together. "But I had a lot more at stake. Your career was already established."

He pulled a face. "Such as it was."

"Let's just agree we are an unbeatable team and leave it at that, shall we?" She leaned forward, kissably close.

He drew back. "I'm sorry I doubted your ability to capture an audience and hold them transfixed." It was difficult to make out his expression in the dark, but his tone was serious.

"That's not important. Only what we accomplished together." She sighed theatrically. "If only we weren't expected to make an appearance at the hotel." She rested her gloved fingers lightly against his lips. "I would far rather our own—more intimate celebration." Surely there could be no misconstruing her meaning.

He pressed a kiss to her fingers. Even through her gloves his lips felt thrillingly warm. "Perhaps that can be arranged. After we fulfill our obligations."

Just then she heard the coach's approach. "Our chariot, has arrived," she said in her best stage voice.

"Your chariot," he said. "I have to join the others at the saloon. It's traditional on opening night for the theater manager to buy the first round. It sets the tone for good luck on subsequent performances."

"In that case, tradition must be upheld," Chandra said in a small voice. "Will you come to the hotel afterwards?"

"Try to keep me away." He kissed her then, too briefly for her liking, but enough to offer a promise of more to come.

The ride up the hill was mercifully short. They arrived at

the hotel before she could sink too far into the mire of her thoughts. Why wasn't she more buoyed up? Riding the wave of her recent success? She'd proven to a theater full of patrons that she could hold her own on stage. Yet, somehow it all felt flat. Was it those other performers, their expressions clearly stating she had a long way to go to become one of them?

Did it really even matter?

She had a wonderful life here in Silver Springs Junction, including The Ophelia where she was guaranteed a stage whenever she wanted. A loving family. And TJ. Surely, he knew how she felt. That she wished to turn their fabricated betrothal into something real. Something where the two of them built a future.

She entered the lobby to rousing applause. Applause that meant nothing without TJ by her side. One of the maids took her cloak and scurried away with it.

Afi, who commanded the room, had pulled in quite a crowd. She wondered if she'd be on the receiving end of the same accolades if she'd fallen flat on her face, then pushed the thought away. No reason to do herself and everyone here a disservice.

She wove her way through the guests amid frequent pauses. Everyone seemed to want a piece of her, so she smiled and nodded her thanks at the nice things they said. From across the room, Callan Douglas sent an approving glance her way. Of course he'd be happy. His investment in the theater was secure. Ryder Lyon doffed his hat as she passed. Of course he would. He'd been talking up The Ophelia from coast to coast. A successful opening was a feather in his cap as well. She hugged her sisters one by one before accepting a warm pat on the back from Selene's husband, Beckett.

Seeing him stand with a loving arm around her sister's

waist, Chandra felt a jolt of envy. Wishing TJ stood next to her, gazing at her as if she'd just hung the moon and polished all the stars. She'd give up the world's most successful stage career to feel secure. To feel loved. She caught sight of Victoria Danford across the room. Now, she understood what her friend had meant. True love was worth any sacrifice.

When she reached Victoria's side, the older gentleman next to the actress greeted her with a warm smile before he clasped her hand with both of his.

"Miss Danford told me of your extraordinary skills, Miss Crawford. And while I know she has an eye for talent when she sees it, even I was a little skeptical that you'd live up to my expectations."

Victoria slapped him playfully on the arm. "Ignore Truman. He has an old fashion way of thinking. That he needs to keep his clients humble."

"It never worked with you, my dear."

"Because I wouldn't have it."

"Sorry," Chandra said, confused by their banter. "I assumed this was your husband."

Victoria laughed. "Heavens to Betsy. Although we have known each other so long we do we act like an old married couple. No. Truman Black was my long-suffering agent when I was on stage."

"Suffering is putting it mildly," he said. "When I met Victoria, I had a full head of hair. Now look at me." They both laughed. Chandra smiled at their good-natured humor as her eyes strayed to the door. Watching for TJ. Wishing he was by her side. She only returned to the conversation when she became aware of Mr. Black addressing her directly. And not for the first time.

"I said, how does that sound to you, Miss Crawford?"

"I'm sorry. My attention strayed momentarily. What was it you asked?"

He exchanged an amused look with Victora. "It seems our poor girl can't believe her ears. I said I would be most happy if you would accompany me back to New York. There are people there you need to meet." He leveled his gaze. "The entertainment industry is on the cusp of change, Miss Crawford. And your performance tonight proves you could be one of those leading the charge."

Victoria nodded encouragingly. "Truman has the ability to open doors for you. *If* that is the life you truly want."

She stiffened as his words sank in. What was wrong with her? She should be bouncing off the walls with joy. Instead, she had a hollow feeling in her tummy. Leave Silver Springs Junction? Leave TJ and The Ophelia?

"When would you want me to go with you?"

"Immediately. Tomorrow."

"Tomorrow? Oh, I couldn't—"

"Why couldn't you?" This from Victoria. "It's all you've talked about since we first met."

"It's—" She floundered. Too much. Too unexpected. Too soon. "It's too sudden. The theater has only just opened. I can't possibly leave TJ to handle everything on his own."

"Did I hear my name?"

She whirled, trying to look welcoming rather than panicked. "TJ. I'm so glad you made it."

He smiled down at her. "I always keep my promises."

"You know Miss Danford. Her companion is Truman Black."

"Congratulations," Mr. Black said, shaking TJ's hand. "The theater is quite something. As is your starring actress."

"I was hardly the star."

"If you're not now, you will be soon." Truman addressed

TJ. "I'm attempting to steal her away. Bribing her with the bright lights of Broadway."

TJ's neutral gaze found hers. "Congratulations. That was always your dream."

She searched his face. "Dreams change."

"An opportunity like this doesn't come along every day," TJ said. "You must take advantage of the opportunity."

Chandra stood rooted to the ground, eyes for TJ alone. "Mr. Black wants me to leave with him tomorrow."

"Tomorrow." TJ's voice faltered slightly, then recovered with a faint smile. A smile that didn't reach his eyes. "No time like the present."

"I was explaining I can't leave on such short notice. Not while you're an act short."

His expression tightened. His eyes grew flinty. "Don't worry about the show. We'll manage." He turned away. "You should go and pack."

"TJ. I—" But he was already gone, shouldering his way through the guests to where the gentlemen stood to one side, whisky glasses in hand.

She turned back to her companions. Victoria was watching her with a concerned expression.

"I'm sorry, Mr. Black. I really can't go tomorrow. If the opportunity is as lucrative as you implied, the bright lights of Broadway will still be there when I'm ready."

"As long as you understand there are no guarantees. It is a very fickle business. They love you one day and hate you the next."

She swallowed a half-laugh, half-sob. It was a feeling she knew all too well. "I appreciate the offer. As well as your confidence in me. Please excuse me."

She worked her way through the room, playing the gracious hostess as she went, pausing by Afi's side long enough for him to introduced her to several businessmen new to the area. There was a hum in the room that had nothing to do with her, and everything to do with the future of Silver Springs Junction. Afi's dream come to fruition. Was it only her whose dream had changed?

"Impressive performance tonight, Miss Crawford."

"Thank you, Mr. Douglas."

"Surely we've known each other long enough that you can call me Callan. After all we're business partners as well as acquaintances."

He might be addressing her but his gaze followed Maia as she conferred with the hotel staff, busy seeing to the guests' needs.

"As you can see, this hotel is my sister's entire world," Chandra said. "I hope the addition of your hotel in the town doesn't threaten that somehow."

Callan shrugged. "No one can have their sole focus on only one thing. Not if they want a full and rewarding life."

"I could not have said it better."

As she left him to join in the small talk between her sisters, her gaze slid in TJ's direction, anxious for the right moment to tell him she was staying.

Minerva tugged on her sleeve in a bid for her attention. "You'll never believe it! Afi is letting me to go Paris."

"Wow!" She hugged her. "That's wonderful news."

"And thanks in part to you," Minerva said.

"Me? I had nothing to do with it. I swear."

"Nonsense. When Afi saw you tonight on stage, something must have clicked. Suddenly he was talking about how much each of us was capable of once our minds were set. He likened you and your stage career to me and my art. Even praised Maia's work here at the hotel, and Selene with the emporium. He said he was sorry for denying me my chance to fully shine. Then he gave me his blessing." Minerva squeezed her hand with excitement. "Did I hear right? You're gong to New York with Mr. Black?"

Who had let that cat out of the bag? "Not exactly. At least not right away."

"TJ said it was all arranged." Minerva blinked. "He didn't even seem sad that you're leaving him behind. Is everything all right between you two?"

"It's complicated," she said. And time for a private chat with Mr. Dirks.

CHAPTER 19

TJ glanced at the guests mingling around the hotel lobby in little clusters. The room resounded with the rise and fall of animated voices. What was he even doing here? He'd been far more comfortable with the performers at the saloon earlier. Folks cut from the same cloth as him. Traveling the country. Sleeping wherever and whenever the opportunity arose. Never calling any one place home.

Once Chandra left, would he still have a shot at running the theater? What would she tell her family about them? That she was coming back? That she'd broken his heart, so be extra nice to him? His jaw clenched at the thought of being little more than a charity case. He tossed back his whisky and set down his glass on a nearby side table. Time to go. Time to remember his place.

He spun so abruptly he collided with Chandra, knocking her off balance. He grabbed her arm to steady her. "Did no one ever tell you not to sneak up on a man who's had a few drinks? He might become suddenly clumsy and knock you off your feet."

"You're never clumsy," she said. "As for knocking me off my feet, that happened the first time I laid eyes on you."

She looked really happy. Due, no doubt, to her leaving. Chasing her dream. As they faced each other, the room, the noise, the guests faded into the background. All his attention centered on the woman before him. "I never touched you, let alone knocked you over."

"Figure of speech," she said lightly. "You told me earlier tonight you always keep your promises."

Lord, what else had he said?

"And I recall one particularly intriguing proposition. After we had both fulfilled our obligations." Her gaze flitted around the room. The guests had noticeably begun to thin out. "Which appears to be now."

He ground the heel of one hand into his eye. "It's been a long day." What had he been thinking earlier? For one, he hadn't known she'd be leaving. At least not right away. No way could he take her back to his makeshift digs at the theater for their first and last night together. She deserved better. And so did he. Losing her would be hard enough. He didn't need to muddy the moment with a night of passion.

She captured his hand in one of hers. It felt small. Feminine. Vulnerable. So why did he feel like the vulnerable one?

Perhaps, because, for the second time in his life, he was being left behind by a woman he loved. First his mother. Now Chandra.

Her tone was teasing. "Don't you think I deserve something to remember you by?"

"You deserve better than me."

She shook her head. "There is no one better." Still holding his hand, she led him from the lobby through to the kitchen, away from prying eyes and up a back stairway.

"Where are we going?"

"There's a room in one of the turrets. We keep it for special occasions."

"Is this a special occasion?"

"I would definitely say this qualifies."

She led the way up a narrow, winding staircase which opened into a room like nothing he'd ever seen. Round in shape, invitingly cozy, with a huge poster bed facing a warmly glowing fireplace. Tapestries draped the stone walls and thick carpet muffled their steps. Even the windows were rounded.

He made his way to one and looked out. The entire town of Silver Springs Junction lay before him like a map in shadow. It was hard to tell where the land ended and the sky began. The occasional light flickered in someone's window, a pale competitor with the star-filled sky.

He turned to find her watching him patiently. So un-Chandra-like to exercise patience. Giving him time to adjust to their surroundings. To them.

Except there was no 'them'.

Conflict warred within. Would one taste be enough? Or only leave him with an eternal hunger for more? Was it even a risk he was willing to take? He opened his mouth to tell her he couldn't do this, couldn't be with her but the words wouldn't come.

"Aren't you going to say anything?"

He reached her side in two long strides. Laid a finger against her lips. "No words. Just memories. Something for us."

Something to remember her by. As if he could ever forget.

He kissed her, softly at first, but her patience had been

short lived. In seconds, a desperate hunger flared between them, fanning the flames of desire that threatened to consume them both. He edged her toward the bed.

He intended to go slow, to take his time, to make it special for her, but she was having none of it. She ripped at his clothing and hers, hands shaking, eyes glittering, as they knelt facing each other. She was beautiful in the firelight. Her skin glowed with dancing flecks of scarlet and gold.

Her hands were all over him, greedily touching him everywhere, testing his control. He caught them with one of his, pressing them to his bare chest. Allowing her to feel the wild racing of his heart. With his free hand he raised her chin to look deeply into her eyes. "I want this to last. To be something you never forget."

She blinked up at him. "I feel like I've waited my entire life for this moment."

As had he. He inhaled shakily, eased her down onto her back. Her bare breasts taunted him to have a taste. Except one taste wasn't enough. And never would be. He gorged himself, wildly dragging his lips from one to the other, back and forth, until she cupped them in her hands and pushed them together, filling his mouth with the pair. Filling his mouth with her.

Reluctantly he abandoned his delightful task to lick and nuzzle his way down her midsection and lower. She tangled her fingers through his hair, encouraging him to continue lower, to find and free that delightful Venus mound of treasures. To continue to plunder her most sensitive areas until she was writhing and screaming and he was filled with the scent and taste of her. Ambrosia a man could die for.

Abruptly she turned tables, straddled his chest and attacked his trousers until she had freed him from his confines. She made a feminine gurgle of pleasure as she touched him, tentatively at first, then with growing confidence. He pressed his lips together, fighting for self-control. Fighting to regain the upper hand. Until she took him into her mouth. Ran her tongue around him, pressed her lips together and sucked.

He pulled back. She faced him wide-eyed. "Did that hurt? I'm so sorry. I didn't know—"

"Shush." He gathered her against him. "I was about to embarrass myself in a way that hasn't happened since I learned better control."

"Oh." She smiled against his chest. "Then I was doing it right."

He tugged her head back so he could absorb her beauty. "Far too right. But there's a lot more to learn about the ways in which a man and woman enjoy each other."

"Oh, good," she said. "We have all night."

A night that would never be enough.

SHE SAT PROPPED against the pillows the next morning watching him dress. A secret smile played with her lips as she recalled the last eight hours. Very little of which had been wasted on sleep.

He stabbed his arms into his shirt and consulted his timepiece before he slipped it into his pocket. "What time is your train?"

"I believe it leaves at eleven."

"You'd best get up and pack."

She pleated the sheet between her fingers. "Please listen to me when I say I don't want to go."

He sat heavily on the edge of the bed. "I hear you. But it's something you must do."

"There will be other opportunities," she said stubbornly.

"You don't know that."

"I don't care if I miss out. I'd rather stay here with you."

He blew out a breath as he rose. Cruel to be kind. "I don't want you here. If you stay, folks will say I only made something of myself because of you. You and your family's wealth." He pulled on his jacket. "We had a deal. The theater debuts, and so do you. After which you travel East while I stay behind acting brokenhearted. That way, your grandfather will feel pity for me and not oust me. At least not right away. Not before I'm established and successful."

"Not ever. Afi drew up a contract."

"We both know contracts can be broken."

"I'll make him promise."

He nodded. "But you will go."

She watched him sadly. He didn't love her. If he did, he'd leap at the chance to have her stay.

"Very well." The fire had gone out sometime in the night. She clambered from bed, shivering as the cool air hit her skin, not at all self-conscious. She hoped he was watching her. Thinking about what he'd be missing. Would he regret sending her away? After a time, would he even remember her? Probably not. She'd be easy to replace with a variety of faceless, nameless females like before.

She sighed heavily, Time to accept that he'd never trust any woman. Never let down his guard enough to love and be loved.

Next time she looked he was gone.

She twisted the emerald ring from her fingers. She'd leave it with Maia. Her sister would see he got it back, along with the others that were still in the hotel safe.

It took longer to pack than she expected. Maia must have spread the word for her sisters and Afi were gathered, solemn-faced, in the lobby when she came downstairs. She dropped her bag so she could hug them each in turn.

"Minerva, dazzle them in Paris. I expect to hear wonderful things come to fruition from your trip abroad."

"Let me know once you get settled in New York so I have somewhere to send my letters," Minerva said.

She nodded. New York. It sounded so lonely. So far away.

She hugged Selene. "Take care of Afi," she whispered in her sister's ear. Selene nodded and swallowed thickly. "You be careful on your own out there."

Maia clung longer than the others. "I'll miss you," Chandra said, once her sister had released her.

Maia nodded and blinked. "I'm looking forward to having my own room all to myself."

"You should have said so sooner." They exchanged a long look.

She turned to say goodbye to Afi, then froze momentarily. Suddenly she saw him through the eyes of a grown woman. He was no longer a young man. She hugged him extra hard. What if this was the last time she saw him?

He gave her a searching look. "I thought you and young Dirks made quite a good team. Took me by surprise, I'll admit, but I'm proud of you. Both of you. Are you sure this is what you want?"

It wasn't, but it was what TJ wanted. Funny how his wants superseded hers.

"Always," she said past the lump in her throat, blinking back the tears. "The theater here was always the means to an end."

Afi shook his head sadly. "Things are changing too fast

for these old bones. Minerva leaving us for Paris. You heading out East."

"You thrive on change," Chandra said. "You've always said it keeps you young."

"Only an old fool would spew such nonsense." He gave her his most serious look. "If they don't treat you right, if things are not to your liking, don't hesitate. You come right back to us. Promise?"

"I promise. I'll write often."

"Don't expect me to write back," he said gruffly. "I despise letter writing." He picked up her valise. "Smithy's waiting on you. I see the others are too." He handed her into the carriage, stood back and gave a brief wave.

"Your grandfather's not coming to see you off?" Truman said.

Victoria patted her hand. "Like most men, he's more sentimental than he lets on. Probably afraid he'll embarrass himself when the waterworks start flowing. How did you and your sisters come up with such an unusual name for him?"

"I believe it started with Maia. Pronouncing grandfather was too much for her young tongue. She had a book about Vikings in which the grandfather was called Afi, so she adopted it to him. The rest of us followed her lead."

"It suits him," Victoria said. "Would you care to stop by the theater?"

Chandra gave her head a quick shake, proud of herself when she didn't even glance that way as they drove past.

The train station was living up to its reputation as a junction. Four or five trains converged on the tracks, coming from and going to various locations east, west and south. The platform was bedlam, but somehow Truman found a porter to take care of their bags and direct them to the right train. Chandra was just about to board when Victoria gripped her arm.

"Your young man is here."

Chandra's heart pounded as she slowly turned, her eyes hungry for the sight of him. Had he changed his mind? But no. He was talking with a man and woman who had vaudeville written all over them. From their traveling costumes to their luggage.

She shrugged. "It looks like TJ's missing act showed up."

Victoria subjected her to that familiar, searching look of hers. Chandra turned away, boarded the train and followed Truman to their seats.

TJ HAD DELIBERATELY TARRIED at the station, hoping to see Chandra. To make sure she really did board, but also so she'd see the other performers had arrived. He no longer needed her.

Hah! No longer needed her. He felt as if a piece of him had been torn from his body. The sooner she was out of his life and out of his mind, the better. He started to guide the couple with him from the station platform when a flash of movement near the hobo camp on the river caught his eye. One of the hobos beckoned to him.

He addressed to his performers. "The theater is just across the way. The door's open. Someone will be there who can show you around. I'll be along shortly." He turned in the opposite direction and made his way from the train platform to the river bank where the hobo watched his approach anxiously. The man gave an acknowledging nod, then darted ahead through the camp before TJ reached him.

He hurried to keep the hobo in sight, weaving his way past makeshift shelters and cooking fires. His heart sank when he saw where they were headed. Buckshot lay unmoving atop his bundle of rags. His old friend was burning up with a fever, his skin an unhealthy red pallor, dotted with beads of sweat. He pulled out his billfold and peeled off a handful of bills that he passed to the first hobo. "Go fetch the doctor. Hurry!"

The man didn't move. TJ sighed. What was he thinking? No doctor would make his way into the camp, no matter who was doing the asking.

"Give me a hand, then. We'll take him there ourselves."

Buckshot groaned as they hoisted him to his feet. He weighed little more than the bundle of rags he used for a bed. Keeping him upright with one hand, TJ grabbed the handles of an old rusted handcart and folded his friend onto it. He and the other hobo managed to push the cart through the camp and up the narrow pathway toward the street.

When they reached the street, Buckshot grabbed him and pulled him down close to listen. He had to put his ear almost atop the other man's lips to make out his words.

"You've got a chance. Take it."

"What?"

"I had a girl once. I let her go. Don't end up like me."

TJ frowned. How did Buckshot know about him and Chandra? Probably from his time spent at the theater, observing more than anyone knew.

Buckshot gave him a frail shove when he moved to grab the handcart handle. His voice was raspy and low. "Go! Before it's too late. Ray will see me to the doc."

TJ heard a train's whistle blow. He looked around. Sure enough, Chandra's train was pulling out of the station. He hesitated, looked over at the two hobos. They were both nodding. Ray inclined his head in the direction of the train.

TJ took a breath and started to run. It had been a long time since he'd jumped aboard a moving train. He hoped he still remembered how.

CHAPTER 20

T hankfully their group was in a private compartment. Chandra didn't think she could have borne the attention from nosy strangers who might have seen her stage debut last night and wanted to talk about it. Any triumph she'd felt in front of the audience paled next to her night spent in TJ's arms.

Truman sat across from her and Victoria, engrossed in a paper he had picked up at the station. Victoria gave her a gentle poke to get her attention. "I recognize that look. It's exclusive to any lucky woman newly in love."

So much for not wearing her heart on her sleeve. She turned to her companion. "Has anyone ever told you you're far too observant?"

"My husband. He views the world through a man's eyes. Very different from those of a woman."

A true statement if she'd ever heard one.

Victoria gave her elbow a squeeze. "Are you sure about this decision, my dear? Everything happened rather suddenly."

She sighed. "You've been telling me for months that I'm ready."

"I only meant ready for the stage. Not necessarily to leave behind everything and everyone you know and love. Such a big step requires much thought and consideration."

"You left everything behind when you moved to White Sulphur Springs. Do you have regrets?"

"Not a one." Victoria's look was direct and unwavering. "But I was embracing love in my life, not running from it."

She lowered her gaze to the decorative piping on her sleeve. "I wanted to stay. After I—I discovered I have feelings for TJ."

Victoria widened her eyes, encouraging her to continue.

"Feelings he doesn't return. Ever since his mother left, he doesn't trust women."

"So, he leaves them before they can leave him."

"Reversed in this case, but yes. He all but pushed me out the door, telling me to have a nice life. Wishing me well."

"And you left. Proving his point. That he was right not trust you with his heart."

"You think if I had stayed—?"

"None of us can predict the future. We can only control our actions in the here and now."

"Are you saying I made a mistake?"

"I think perhaps you were a little hasty. And so was he. He knew this was your dream. A dream he didn't want you to sacrifice for him."

"You're right." She half stood, panicking. "I've made a dreadful mistake. I must get off immediately."

Victoria sat back with a self-satisfied smile. "You'll have to wait until we reach White Sulphur Springs. But there should be a train headed back to the junction before long."

"And I can get back before it's too late."

The newspaper rustled as Truman lowered it to his lap. He'd obviously been listening to their conversation. "I can't say I'm not disappointed, Chandra. But Victoria is right. One must listen to one's heart."

She took a breath. Renewed energy coursed through her as if a huge boulder had been lifted. A reprieve. A second chance to make things right. She smiled, imagining TJ's surprise when he saw her.

OLD INSTINCTS KICKED IN. Keeping one eye out for any conductors who might ask to see his ticket, TJ moved from train car to train car, searching for Chandra. He'd been trying so hard to act like he didn't notice her earlier, that he'd not paid attention to useful details such as the color of her travelling cloak and whether or not she wore a hat.

The passengers were a mixed lot. It was easy to pick out the businessmen in their dark suits and fancy hats, or the salesmen with their cases of wares. He saw men down on their luck, no doubt having called it quits in the prospecting fields, next to broken down cowboys who'd look more at home on a horse than a train. But no Chandra.

He reached the front of the train before he realized his mistake. Chandra and her companions wouldn't be found here in the common areas. They'd be out of sight in some private compartment. Behind closed doors. Far tricker to access.

He retraced his steps to the private compartments and stopped in front of the first door, took a breath and quietly opened the door a crack to peer inside. An outraged feminine squeal greeted him and he closed the door quickly before the squeal escalated and brought the conductor running.

Hearing someone approach, he quickly stepped into a shadowy alcove between compartments. He held his breath as a uniformed worker carrying a tray with a silver tea service passed by. He waited till the fellow was well out of sight before he tried the next door and saw a family on their knees in the midst of prayer time. They turned their heads his way in unison, no doubt disappointed he wasn't The Almighty come to join their prayer group.

With a murmured apology he shut the door and moved along the corridor to the next one. No luck there either. As he reached to try the next door, he was nearly mowed over by a small contingent of passengers coming at him from all directions.

He hadn't realized the train had slowed down in preparation to stop. He stepped into an alcove identical to the one he'd sheltered in earlier, just missing being swept along by the sea of disembarking passengers. He squinted at the station sign. White Sulphur Springs was obviously a popular destination. Glancing out the window, he did a double-take.

Blast it all! Chandra and Victoria Danford were on the platform alongside a distinguished older gentleman. TJ raced down the corridor toward the exit. He heard a shout behind him, but didn't stop. The whistle blew. The train started to move just as he flung himself down the steps and onto the platform. He stumbled, lost his footing, and landed hard. He lay there for a second, the breath knocked from his lungs. He must be losing his edge. He'd never fallen from a moving train in all the time he'd ridden the rails looking for his father.

He picked himself up and dusted himself off, aware of curious eyes turned his way.

"I say. Are you all right?" called the porter.

"Nothing bruised but my ego," TJ said. He turned to where he'd last seen Chandra but the platform was empty. She was with Victoria Danford. He'd find her.

He made his way through the station and onto the street out front. Carriages and people on foot moved past with purpose. He looked both ways. And froze. For there she was. Staring at him as if seeing a ghost.

He stood stock still, afraid if he rushed to her side he might scare her away. Chasing her away once had been enough.

"Hello, Chandra."

She gave her head a dainty shake, as if in disbelief. "Victoria said she thought that was you, but I didn't believe her."

He took a step closer. "You got off. I thought you were going all the way to New York with Miss Danford's agent."

She glanced down at the ground, then back up at him. "What are you doing here?"

He took that as his cue to close the distance between them. He'd feel far more sure of himself if he could pull a coin from behind her ear and make her laugh. But this was no laughing matter. This was the real thing. The biggest risk of his life. Of his heart. Risking everything he believed in; everything he was.

"I came for you."

"For me? But how—"

"I was scouring the train looking for you. Even interrupted a couple in the middle of a tryst. Then I spotted you on the platform and barely managed to leap off in the nick of time."

He watched a muscle work in her delicate throat. She

appeared to be having trouble swallowing. Watching the play of emotions across her face, something inside him softened, like a rose that has finally felt the sun. "Your turn."

She took a shuddering breath. "I realized I'd left something behind. Something far too valuable to leave without." She reached for his hands. Hers were trembling. "You."

He pulled her to him. She threw her arms around his neck as if she'd never let him go. "I know you told me to go. I'm hoping you didn't mean it. Not fully." She pulled back. "The fact that you came after me. Does that mean—?"

"That I came to the identical conclusion as you? Yes, my love. I want to be where you are. Wherever that may be."

She exhaled breathily. "I don't care, as long as I can be with you."

He kissed her, gently at first, then with greater hunger and urgency as the meaning of what she said sank in. A future. Their future.

He had no idea how long they stood there, mindless of the giggles and amused chuckles from passersby, until suddenly the air was pierced by a loud whistle. He tensed. Slowly they stepped apart, his arm around her shoulders, her arm snugging his middle. He opened his mouth to say he'd never let her go again, when the whistle sounded again, closer this time.

"I don't believe it." He pointed as his father's caravan pulled to a stop across the street. His father held the reins, a woman beside him. Both of them were waving and grinning like mad fools.

He blinked. Was he only imagining his father and mother together like in the old days? His grip tightened on Chandra. She, at least, was real. She moved closer. Somehow, without him saying a word, she knew. They exchanged a long look. She nodded. He let out a breath he hadn't even

THE MAGICIAN

known he was holding, before they crossed the street and approached the pair.

Silence stretched between the two couples. Finally, he asked, "What brings you this way?"

His father inclined his head toward his companion. "We heard about the theater. Nothing would do for your ma but to come see her boy with her own eyes."

TJ's fingers clenched on Chandra's shoulders as he shifted his gaze to his mother. She'd hardly changed. Her hair was threaded with silver and her face had matured. But those laughing black eyes were the same as his. Her contagious smile exactly as he remembered.

"We're headed to Silver Springs Junction if you'd like a lift," she said. "Shall we three climb in the back and let your father drive? I expect you have questions. I hope I have answers."

TJ looked down at Chandra. "We can wait for the next train if you'd prefer."

Chandra gave her head a quick, dismissive shake. "I'd like nothing more than the chance to get to know your mother."

He clung to Chandra as his mother climbed down. Was the best day of his life about to get better? Or take a turn for the worst? His mother hovered near them, her movements hesitant until Chandra reached out and pulled her into their embrace. He sighed deeply, the arms of the two women he loved wrapped around him. Eventually he took a step back without letting go of either of them.

"I'm sure TJ has lots of questions, but mine gets answered first. What does TJ stand for?"

His mother smiled. "Didn't he tell you?"

He rolled his eyes. *Here we go.*

"Tag Jaxon. Tag is Irish for handsome. Jaxon means son

of Jack." She pointed to her husband. "Handsome son of Jack."

Chandra laughed up at him. "It suits you perfectly."

He shook his head. "Why do I feel I'm going to rue the day you two met?"

"You won't," Chandra said cheekily. "Because it's also the day you and I truly found each other."

His mother tapped him on the chest with her forefinger. "Don't ever lose each other the way your father and I did. Cherish every moment."

He took Chandra's hand and felt underneath her glove for the ring he had placed on her finger. "Don't worry about that. I'm just glad you'll be here to see us wed."

Chandra's eyes lit up. "Yes," she said. "It's high time we set the date."

Stay tuned for Book 3 of the Spinsters, *The Drifter*, Minerva's story. Coming in early 2025.

AFTERWORD

Thanks for reading *The Magician*. You might not know how important reader reviews are, but they mean a lot.

Review wherever you purchased *The Magician* or on Goodreads or BookBub.

Just a short sentence saying you enjoyed the book goes a long way with new readers and puts a smile on this author's face.

And please keep in touch

Website: KathleenLawless.com
Facebook: facebook.com/kathleenlawlessnovels
Instagram: instagram.com/kathleenflawless
TikTok: tiktok.com/@kathleenflawless

Sign up for my VIP reader newsletter to receive updates, special giveaways and fan-priced offers. http://eepurl.com/bVosbı

ALSO BY KATHLEEN LAWLESS

Sweet Western Historical Romance

THE SPINSTER TAKES A GROOM

The Gambler

The Magician

Western Historical Romance

Grace's Folly

Anora's Pride

Callie's Honor

Maddy's Fugitive

Widows, Babies and Brides - Box Set of the 4 Books

Sweet Western Historical Romance

SEVEN BRIDES FOR SEVEN BROTHERS SERIES

Brody's Bride - Book 1

Bradley's Bride - Book 2

Braydon's Bride - Book 3

Blake's Bride - Book 4

Bishop's Bride - Book 5

Barron's Bride - Book 6

Benjamin's Bride - Book 7

Seven Brides for Seven Brothers Box Set 1 - Prequel & Books 1 to 3

Seven Brides for Seven Brothers Box Set 2 - Books 4 to 7

Sweet Western Historical Romance

WIDOWS OF THE WILD WEST

Hope

Janie

Sweet Western Historical Romance

MAIL ORDER BRIDES

Mail Order Olivia

Mail Order Rachel

Mail Order Martina

A Bride for Shane

A Bride for Riley

A Bride for Weston

Mail Order Noelle

Chelsea's Choice

Lila: Rescue Me Mail Order Brides

Here Come the Brides Volume 1

Here Come the Brides Volume 2

Sweet Contemporary Romance

Frannie (Always a Bridesmaid)

Baxter (Last Man Standing)

Blue Sky Island

One Cinderella Spring

One Stolen Summer

One Fantasy Fall

One Wondrous Winter

Sweet Christmas Romance Novellas

Holly's Wish

No Groom at the Inn

Women's Fiction

Fabulous at Fifty

Romantic Suspense

Final Heat

Afterburn

Steamy Historical Romance

Taboo

Unmasked

Reckless Rogues - Box Set of the 2 Books

Steamy Contemporary Romance

SECRET SEDUCTIONS

Her Untamed Cowboy - Book 1

Her Undercover Cowboy - Book 2

Her Unwilling Cowboy - Book 3

Who Needs a Cowboy! - Book 4

Intimate Strangers

For a complete book list visit KathleenLawless.com

To be the first to hear about Kathleen's new releases, special fan pricing sales, and also receive a free book, sign up for her VIP Reader Newsletter at http://eepurl.com/bVosbI

ABOUT THE AUTHOR

USA Today Bestselling Author, Kathleen Lawless, blames a misspent youth watching Rawhide, Maverick and Bonanza for her fascination with cowboys, which doesn't stop her from creating a wide variety of interests and occupations for her many alpha male heroes.

With over 50 published novels to her credit, she enjoys pushing the boundaries of traditional romance into historical romance, contemporary romance, romantic suspense and women's fiction.

She makes her home in the Pacific Northwest and loves to hear from her readers.

Sign up for Kathleen's VIP Reader Newsletter to receive updates, special giveaways and fan-priced offers. http://eepurl.com/bVosb1

KathleenLawless.com

goodreads.com/kathleenlawless

bookbub.com/authors/kathleen-lawless

facebook.com/kathleenlawlessnovels

instagram.com/kathleenflawless

tiktok.com/@kathleenflawless